"You can't ho... responsible..."

Sabrina struggled a... know how my fathe... life! You can't blame me for things he did before I was even old enough to talk—"

"Silence!" He cut her off curtly, his voice vibrant with anger. "Don't ever plead with me, Sabrina. You will be trampled into the ground."

"But if you imagine that I can be held responsible for my father's crimes—"

"I don't think any such thing," he snapped. "But you will conduct yourself with dignity in this house, or as surely as your father eclipsed my family, I *will* humiliate and destroy you."

"No." She faced him with tight lips. "You'll never do that to me, Leo L'Aquila. *Never!*"

Books by Madeleine Ker

HARLEQUIN ROMANCE
2595—VOYAGE OF THE MISTRAL
2636—THE STREET OF THE FOUNTAIN
2709—ICE PRINCESS
2716—HOSTAGE

HARLEQUIN PRESENTS
642—AQUAMARINE
656—VIRTUOUS LADY
672—PACIFIC APHRODITE
699—THE WINGED LION
739—WORKING RELATIONSHIP
778—OUT OF THIS DARKNESS
795—FIRE OF THE GODS

These books may be available at your local bookseller.

Don't miss any of our special offers. Write to us at the
following address for information on our newest releases.

Harlequin Reader Service
P.O. Box 52040, Phoenix, AZ 85072-2040
Canadian address: P.O. Box 2800, Postal Station A,
5170 Yonge St., Willowdale, Ont. M2N 6J3

Hostage

Madeleine Ker

Harlequin Books

TORONTO • NEW YORK • LONDON
AMSTERDAM • PARIS • SYDNEY • HAMBURG
STOCKHOLM • ATHENS • TOKYO • MILAN

Original hardcover edition published in 1985
by Mills & Boon Limited

ISBN 0-373-02716-8

Harlequin Romance first edition September 1985

Copyright © 1985 by Madeleine Ker.
Philippine copyright 1985. Australian copyright 1985.

All rights reserved. Except for use in any review, the reproduction or utilization
of this work in whole or in part in any form by any electronic, mechanical
or other means, now known or hereafter invented, including xerography,
photocopying and recording, or in any information storage or retrieval system,
is forbidden without the permission of the publisher, Harlequin Enterprises
Limited, 225 Duncan Mill Road, Don Mills, Ontario, Canada M3B 3K9. All the
characters in this book have no existence outside the imagination of the
author and have no relation whatsoever to anyone bearing the same name
or names. They are not even distantly inspired by any individual known
or unknown to the author, and all the incidents are pure invention.

The Harlequin trademarks, consisting of the words HARLEQUIN ROMANCE
and the portrayal of a Harlequin, are trademarks of Harlequin Enterprises
Limited; the portrayal of a Harlequin is registered in the United States Patent
and Trademark Office and in the Canada Trade Marks Office.

Printed in U.S.A.

CHAPTER ONE

HE was standing in the snow as she came out of the Albany with Roderigo Gomez.

A tall, dark figure on the other side of the street, not noticeable enough to do more than give her the tiniest flash of unease before she looked away.

She drew her fur closer around her, and shivered slightly as she glanced up at the still-falling flakes with eyes that were a deep blue, made all the more striking by long black lashes and hair that rivalled her sable coat in its lustrous blackness.

'Snow again,' she sighed as Roderigo took her arm. 'Thank you for a very pleasant afternoon, Roderigo.' She knew that the invitation had been made out of courtesy, not warmth, and she'd accepted with foreboding, as she always did. The opulent lunch in the walnut-panelled chambers had been strained, and made unhappy for her by too many memories of her father. There had been the usual succession of men who had known and hated him, yet who seemed to feel obliged to express unctuous sympathies to his only daughter. Behind the polite lies, as always, she had sensed their fear. Fear that Simon Westlake's youthful daughter was going to wield the same ruthless power in the City that her father had exercised for almost fifteen years. What the hell was she

going to do about that? How did you follow a
father you'd always feared and hated? She
couldn't help the momentary dread that time—
and the vast wealth her father had left her—
might turn her, too, into a personality as
rapacious as Simon Westlake had been. Then she
rejected the thought passionately.

'*Never*,' she whispered.

'What was that?' Roderigo asked, eyebrows
lifting.

'Nothing. I just hate the way they come up to
me like that,' she told him as they descended the
marble stairs. 'Like vassals greeting the war-
lord's heir.'

'Simon was a powerful man, Sabrina.' Roderigo
Gomez's silver hair and sallow features had
always reminded her of a retired military dictator.
'It is natural that your father's rivals should now
wish to ingratiate themselves with his daughter,
no?'

'They loathe me,' she said in a low voice,
remembering the sly antagonism in those well-fed,
prosperous faces.

'Only because you are more powerful than they
are,' Roderigo smiled.

She knew that wasn't all, though. 'Not just for
that,' she said, shaking her head. 'My father must
have hurt most of them in some way or another
during his life. They're wondering whether I'm
going to turn out the same.'

'You judge your late father too harshly,'
Roderigo said urbanely, as though he hadn't
noticed the bitterness in her voice. The gleaming
black limousine pulled up silently in front of

them in the crisp snow, as sleekly efficient as everything else her father had left behind. Inwardly, Sabrina resolved to get rid of the sinister, hearse-like thing as soon as possible, and insist that she be allowed to drive her own red Mini.

Roderigo pulled the door open for her; but as she prepared to step into the plush interior, some sixth sense made her look up again at the man across the street, who hadn't moved from where he stood.

Her heart contracted sharply as she met the eyes that were studying her. Cloudy grey eyes, almost shockingly beautiful in their intensity. Eyes that glittered mockingly in a tanned, fiercely authoritative face. Roderigo, noticing her sudden stiffness, looked up also.

The man who was watching them with such a sardonic glint in those splendid eyes raised his soft black hat in a greeting which conveyed as much ironic mockery as politeness. Another of her father's enemies? Sabrina studied his face quickly, noting the commanding, passionate mouth, the hard lines of cheekbones and chin. Everything about him spoke of arrogant power—even the way he stood in the snow, one fist on his hip, thrusting back the beautifully-cut and obviously foreign coat to reveal an equally superb charcoal suit. He simply stood there, smiling.

No, not smiling. Only his eyes were amused—and amused in a way that was not light enough to be called a smile.

Sabrina nodded icily in reply to the greeting and slipped into the car. Who the hell did he think he was? Through the tinted glass she could still see him, his pose relaxed and yet somehow indefinably threatening, the darkness of his elegant clothes relieved only by the white silk scarf at his neck.

'Who is that man?' she asked Roderigo quietly as he got in beside her.

'I've never seen him before.'

'He's frightening,' she said, still fascinated and angered by the dark, waiting figure. 'He's laughing at us!'

'Let him do as he pleases,' Roderigo shrugged. He glanced sharply out of the window, then turned to Sabrina. 'Would you like to go back to Winfields?'

'A little later,' she decided. 'Can we drop by at the Westlake tower? I'd like to see William Cattermole.'

'Of course.' He rapped on the glass panel behind the driver. 'The tower, please.'

But Sabrina turned in her seat to continue watching as the car pulled away. There was now a smile, she was sure, on that cruel mouth, and for an instant he was almost Satanic, staring after the car with brooding grey eyes as though he could pierce the tinted, armoured glass and touch Sabrina's soul. She knew so little of men, was so ill-equipped to understand or deal with them. Even a casual glance like that could set her heart pounding like a hunted doe's. He turned, and walked with lithe swiftness up the marble steps to the glass doors of the hotel.

'I've had about enough of this hostility that follows me everywhere.' Sabrina turned forward

and shrugged the sable off her shoulders as
though it had suddenly begun to suffocate her.
'It's been haunting me ever since I inherited my
father's . . .' She struggled for a word, and found
one with bitterness. 'My father's *empire*.'

'At least you look the part of an empress,'
Roderigo smiled. The green dress she wore
hugged her slender figure with a severe elegance,
and a diamond as big as an almond glittered in
the cool hollow of her throat.

The image was so exactly that of a rich and
powerful young beauty that she might have been
a clever actress playing the part. But she'd
realized long since that when meeting the men
who ran Westlake it was essential to dress the
part of Simon Westlake's daughter, no matter
how remote that part might be from her true
nature. Diamonds and furs, the cool green dress
cut low enough to emphasise her womanhood—
that was today's image. Intriguing and yet
definitely forbidding.

'Did that man upset you?' Roderigo asked,
watching her through narrowed eyes as he lit a
cigarillo.

'A little,' she admitted, beginning to regret
having shown any emotion in front of Roderigo.
He'd been her father's second-in-command for
twenty years, and she didn't trust him a
millimetre.

'Put him out of your mind,' he advised
urbanely. 'There will be many such insolent men,
fascinated by Sabrina Westlake.' He puffed
reflectively, hooded eyes on her figure. 'You are
more beautiful than ever today, my dear.'

'Thank you,' she nodded coolly.

'I take it the dress is your own design?'

She nodded indifferently. The sophisticated couture, along with the liquidly glossed lips and the immaculate make-up, were a kind of armour as well as a disguise. They enabled her to survive, somewhere deep inside the exquisite image, until she could work out a way of escaping from the nightmare of being Simon Westlake's heir. If Roderigo said she looked beautiful, that meant her armour was intact. Nothing more. That was one thing money could do, she thought drily. It bought you the best armour available.

She glanced at Roderigo's face as he turned his attention to the briefcase beside him. Now, as often before, she had the feeling that he was more than half-aware of her real feelings about the Westlake Corporation. As her father's lifelong vice-chairman, he could have few delusions about the way in which she and her mother had suffered, victims of her father's cruelty and all-encompassing greed for power. He knew, of course, that she had never loved her father, that she had always hated the ruthless principles upon which Simon Westlake had based his life and business methods. He might suspect that inheriting the Westlake empire had been the very last thing that Sabrina expected or wanted.

And that suspicion, she knew, would make Roderigo hungry for power.

'These are the details of next Friday's meeting,' he said, passing her a sheet of paper. 'But of course you already know the main topics on the agenda—the necessity of securing another

Government defence contract, the problem of competition from other firms, notably Cressida Industrial, and a decision on the Tyneside firm.' Sabrina nodded again, studying the sheet. Over the past months, she hadn't attempted to contradict Roderigo once. Not directly. Her father's death had left her all-powerful—yet it was Roderigo who actually ran the company, and who knew more about it than anyone else. Sabrina's three years' experience running her own fashion design business had scarcely prepared her to understand the operations of a giant electronics empire.

Which didn't stop her from having some firm opinions about the Westlake Corporation. On the matter of the closure of the Tyneside factory, for example, her own views were diametrically opposed to Roderigo's.. She wondered how he was going to take her opposition.

Roderigo wanted Westlake badly, she knew that. She could simply hand the reins over to him, and let him run the show. That would enable her to go back to her beloved design project, currently being run in Manchester by her friend, Clarissa Taylor, and never have another worry again. To be wealthy without the responsibility of Westlake or the taint of her father's personality on everything she touched.

If only she could get rid of her absurd sense of responsibility to Westlake's many thousands of employees! But no matter how much she wanted to escape from the ugliness of being his heir, she couldn't simply shake off the thought of those lives. She owed them something more than that.

And no matter how easy it would be to hand

Westlake over to Roderigo Gomez, she simply didn't trust him enough. He was as selfish a man as her father had been, and she hated the thought of her future resting so completely in his hands. She was essentially alone. She'd always had few friends, and almost no men-friends, and she'd long since realised that quarter was neither given nor asked in this life.

It was a very tight cleft stick. Well, tomorrow afternoon's board-meeting was going to give her a better insight into Roderigo Gomez's nature. Maybe her position would be a little clearer then.

She looked out at the snowy London streets. That cruel, laughing man in the snow! Those dark eyes had seared into hers, leaving an unease behind that reminded her of just how hated her father had been. Her trained eye told her that the cut of those superb clothes had been foreign, perhaps Italian. Another victim of Simon Westlake's greed? There had been a rapier-like poise about his body, a steel blade aimed taut and unwavering at the heart. Whose heart?

'I wonder who that strange man was?' she asked, almost to herself.

Roderigo smiled with dry lips.

'Perhaps,' he said gently, 'he was the Devil himself.'

William Cattermole met them in Simon Westlake's luxurious office, now officially Sabrina's. As the wise old lawyer who presided over the Corporation's financial dealings, he had so far had more to do with Sabrina than any of the other board members who had unexpectedly found themselves under the command of a beautiful twenty-two-year-old woman. William, unlike some of the others, had accepted Sabrina without obvious dismay or condescension. In return, Sabrina found that she trusted the unambitious and kindly William far more than any of the others, including Roderigo Gomez.

'With regard to item seven on the agenda for Friday,' William said to Sabrina after the greetings were dispensed with. 'Competition from Cressida Industrial and other electronics firms. There's something I think you should hear about before the meeting.'

'Go ahead,' she nodded. Sabrina had long since realised to her amusement that William disguised the sharp intelligence of his eyes behind gold-rimmed glasses which gave him a benevolently Pickwickian air. Now he took the spectacles off, and revealed the face of a tired old man.

'I've just received some very serious information. I believe that Cressida are shortly going to make an offer for Westlake.'

'*What?*' Roderigo leaned forward in angry surprise. 'An offer for Westlake? You're joking, William. No one—but no one—has the muscle to take over Westlake!'

'Nevertheless,' William said gently, 'I have it on certain authority that within the next few weeks Cressida Industrial are going to make a bid for control of Westlake.'

Feeling extremely feminine and out of place in the throne-like armchair behind her father's intimidating desk, Sabrina smiled. 'Are you saying that Cressida want to buy this corporation, William?'

'Exactly that.'

'Isn't that rather unlikely?'

'It's insane,' Roderigo snorted.

'Insane or not,' the company lawyer said quietly, 'we're going to have to face it. In fact, there are straws in the wind already. There's been an unprecedented run on Westlake shares for the past week. The Accounts Department noticed it first. At first I was inclined to dismiss it—but the run has been sustained ever since last Monday. Our shares have climbed eighteen points over the past two days. There's every sign that shareholders are taking advantage of the rise to cash in on at least some of their holdings.'

Roderigo's cold brown eyes narrowed. 'A rise in our shares can only be good news for us. Between us, Sabrina and I own thirty per cent of the stock. Simon saw to that.'

'Cressida only need fifty-one percent to dominate this corporation,' William said.

'Rubbish,' Roderigo sneered at William. His urbane good manners towards her, Sabrina noticed, evaporated when he came to deal with other board-members. 'The whole notion is ridiculous. *No one* has the capital or the strength to try a take-over on the Westlake Corporation.'

'Cressida is a young giant. It would be ridiculous indeed to underestimate their power— or the brilliance of the men who run it.'

Oh for the simplicities of her conferences with Clarissa! She was a long way out of her depth in this sort of conversation. 'So what are you saying?' she asked William gently, knowing that he was subtly trying to give her a message.

'I'm saying that there may be one hell of a storm ahead. With all due respect to the Chairman, Cressida International are very, very big. And very hungry. They have almost fathomless reserves of capital, crying out for a home. And my sources tell me that Westlake is just about the right size piggy-bank for their excess millions.'

'Westlake, a piggy-bank?' Roderigo spat out. 'You seriously mean to tell me that some tinpot foreign company could come along and put us all out of a job overnight? Don't make me laugh, Cattermole!'

'I advise you to check Cressida's listings,' William replied, and she noticed a slight flush of anger in his cheeks now.

'You're getting old, William,' Roderigo retorted with a harsh laugh. 'You're seeing burglars under the bed.' His scorn reminded Sabrina so sharply of her father that she turned to him with real anger in her deep blue eyes.

'May I remind you that I am the owner, Roderigo,' she said icily. 'If William thinks there's something I should know, then I want to hear it.' Roderigo's expression was venomous for a second; then, with an elaborate courtesy that showed he was deeply offended, he gestured to the lawyer to proceed. Damn! She hated having to clash swords, no matter how trivially, with the formidable Corporation Chairman like that— especially as she was going to oppose him again during the board meeting. She kept her face cool as she turned back to William Cattermole. 'You say there may be a take-over bid ahead. But

Westlake is a strong company. Is Cressida really that big?'

'Oh, they could do it,' William said mildly, ignoring Roderigo's hostile glance. 'If they really wanted to.'

'They'd have a fight to the death on their hands,' Roderigo put in sharply.

'Whose death?' William asked mildly. 'Theirs or ours?' He looked back at Sabrina. 'Sabrina, I simply want to make it clear that since your father's death there have been a lot of very powerful guns aimed at this Corporation. We can't afford to ignore even the slightest warning.'

'Cressida,' she said thoughtfully. As if she didn't have enough troubles on her plate! The last thing she wanted was to find herself with a take-over bid on her hands just as she was trying to find a way out of the golden cage her father's death had locked her into. She thought with a wistful flash how rewardingly simple life had been running the design shop. Those three years had been among the happiest of her life, a period when at last she seemed to have escaped from under the shadow of her father's presence. Now, ironically, his death had cast that same darkness over her life again. 'Thank you, William,' she nodded. 'I'd like to hear your views on this. Can we meet to talk about it—say Thursday?'

'Of course.'

'Then let me take you to dinner,' she offered, 'and you can tell me what you think. Claridges? At eight?'

'Thursday at eight suits me fine,' William nodded, avoiding the Chairman's eyes. Roderigo's

expression was bitter. Sabrina had deliberately
excluded him from the invitation, but she needed
to hear what William had to say without his
overbearing presence there. If he didn't want to
listen, she did. 'And now,' she said coolly,
picking up her gloves, 'if you'll be kind enough
to call the car, Roderigo, I want to get back to
Winfields this afternoon.'

On Sunday morning, as usual, she made time for
an hour or two's riding. The only good thing
about Winfields, as far as she was concerned, was
that it was in the country, among fields and
woods that gave her soul rest. For the past three
years Sabrina had felt that her home was in
Manchester, where she'd started Phoenix Design
after she'd left university. From a tiny beginning
in a rented house, Phoenix had gathered strength,
until they'd been able to afford a small city
boutique, and had started marketing their designs
in other big cities. Within a few years, Phoenix
was going to be doing well. Yet since her father's
death she'd been taken away from all that and
thrust into a succession of alien environments—
the great house at Winfields that was now hers,
visits to London and the glass tower on the
Thames, tours of inspection around Westlake
factories across the country.

   She'd never liked Winfields. The oppressively
grandiose old house among the trees was another
of her father's possessions that Sabrina had made
up her mind to get rid of as soon as decently
possible. She turned in the saddle to glance back
at it across the fields. So typical of his style, she

thought wryly; a tasteless Victorian palace meant to amplify his own arrogant nature! The house she and her mother had shared in Cumbria had been roomy and airy, but it had been a house of tragedy for Sabrina, and after three years in the neat flat she'd rented in Manchester after her mother's death, Winfields had seemed over-poweringly large to her.

The only pleasure she'd found there had been the stables, and the big bay stallion her father had bought but never ridden, Criterion. She patted the horse's neck, and trotted him across the meadow. She'd resolved at her mother's funeral never to take another penny from her father, and had launched Phoenix as soon as her grief had subsided enough for her to cope with the new venture. But despite her love of riding, she'd never made enough money in three years to feel that she could indulge in a horse. She'd contented herself with riding-school horses and hired horses—which made Criterion and his splendidly smooth gait doubly tempting!

Across the meadow, she let the horse have his head, revelling in the crisp wintry air and the exhilaration of speed. Big money and big business had little appeal for a woman who'd been exposed to their most ruthless face all her life. She was going to have to get out of this world before it destroyed her . . .

But it was delicious to have what looked like the whole of Berkshire to herself; the snow still lying in the fields made the world seem neat, uncomplicated.

Hoofbeats made her look up. Another rider

was visible through the leafless trees at the end of the field. Not wanting company on this beautiful morning, Sabrina turned Criterion's head aside, and cantered him down to the stream that marked the boundary of Winfields' land. Hidden in a little spinney, she watched the icy waters tumble over the stones, and waited for the horseman to ride by.

But he didn't. To her mingled anger and dismay, she heard the sound of his horse's hooves crunching through the snow towards her hiding-place. Some inquisitive farmer's son, she cursed, with nothing better to do than play hide and seek on a Sunday morning. Resentful at having to flee, she urged Criterion over the stream, and jumped him clumsily over a small hedge; then galloped as fast as she dared across the next field, and turned to look back. She bit her lip hard as she saw that he was coming after her, a man riding beautifully on a dark horse. Should she wait, and outface him? No, she thought, wheeling Criterion round, damn him! She'd made enough of a fool of herself already.

The sound of the hooves behind her was infuriating as she rode hard towards the little wood half a mile away. If she could reach the cover of the trees before he caught up with her, she could maybe lose him there. Her skin had begun to prickle with perspiration under her jeans and anorak. She'd been trying to avoid the rich young men of this neighbourhood ever since she'd moved into her father's house. Their upper-middle-class wooing had been infinitely tedious, especially to someone as unsure of her position and future as Sabrina.

This, by the way he rode, would be Harvey Wilkerson, who was the idiotic son of the local magistrate. He lived for nothing but hunting, and looked and talked like something out of *Brideshead Revisited*.

The ground was frozen in places, and it was a gruelling ride. Criterion's well-oiled stride broke up on the uneven soil, and she jolted painfully three or four times, knocking the breath out of her lungs. She was panting and unsteady as she approached the wood, and the pursuing hoofbeats seemed only a shadow behind her now. Panic and fury made her careless, and she had to grab at the saddle as the big stallion stumbled heavily in a rut, and almost sent her flying over his back. By the time she'd recovered her balance, the horseman had wheeled in front of Criterion, and was blocking her way. She shook a strand of wet black hair off her cheek, gasping for breath, and glared at her pursuer.

'My compliments on a spectacular ride,' he said in a deep, velvety voice. Her eyes widened into shocked blue pools.

'*You!*' It was the man from the Albany, his dark eyes glittering as he smiled, his nostrils flaring with the recent exertion. 'You were staring at me outside the Albany last week,' she panted, anger mingling with fear inside her. 'Why are you hunting me like this?'

'For pleasure,' he replied calmly. The face which smiled insolently down at her was undeniably splendid. There was authority in that mouth, yet in the full lower lip lurked a hint of volcanic passion. A capacity for powerful emotion which would be all the more fierce for the strength of character that was evident in the stormy grey eyes, the level black brows, and the hard, masculine lines of cheekbones and chin. Sabrina stared into the eagle's eyes, grey flecked with amber, and tried to quiet Criterion's uneasy shivering. The two horses panted clouds of steam into the cold air.

'Who are you?' she demanded, wishing she weren't quite so isolated with this formidable pursuer.

He made a mocking bow. 'Your enemy, madame—at your service.'

'My enemy?' she repeated, startled into stammering. 'Why—why my enemy?'

He shrugged, not taking his bright eyes off her. 'Why is the eagle the lamb's enemy?'

The dangerous sexuality in his mockery had the effect of disturbing her even more. He was taller than she, and she was acutely aware of the unspoken aggression in the poise of his body, threatening and yet graceful. He sat the beautiful mare as though he were welded to the saddle, the ruthless grip of his thighs visible in the muscles that strained the whipcord of his jodphurs. His rough Arran sweater emphasised the breadth of his chest, but his boots were supple and skin-tight.

'Well, I'm glad to have afforded you a morning's sport,' she said shortly. Who the hell was he? Her eyes probed his angrily, then she slipped off Criterion, and ran her hands down the horse's trembling legs. A fetlock was ominously

swollen, and when she led him a few paces, the
stallion was limping badly. 'You've made me
sprain my horse's leg,' she accused bitterly.

'You were the one who rode him into the
ditch,' he pointed out.

'You chased me,' she retorted. Being on
horseback gave him a commanding presence
over her. A man with that face and body would
conquer easily; that crisp black hair was a
brazen invitation to female fingers, and the
combination of threat and sensuality in his
manner would set hearts fluttering anywhere.
For God's sake, she thought agitatedly, why
does this Captain Blood have to call himself my
enemy? Is this some kind of sexual come-on?
'What am I going to do with Criterion?' she
asked miserably. 'He can barely walk—and he
needs his leg bandaged up as soon as possible,
thanks to you.'

'In that case,' he purred, 'you will have to
throw yourself upon my mercy.' He held out a
hand. 'Give me the bridle.' She hesitated, then
put Criterion's bridle into his hand. He looped it
round his own left wrist, then held out his right
hand to her again. 'Come.'

'Come where?' she asked suspiciously. This
was the kind of man she automatically branded
M.C.P.—Male Chauvinist Pig. Arrogant, strong,
perhaps dangerous. He stooped, his fingers
closing like steel around her arm, and she
screamed sharply as he swung her up on to his
own saddle. For an ungainly minute, she
struggled—and then found herself sitting between
those hard thighs, her back pressed against his

chest. 'Set me down,' she commanded, her face scarlet with embarrassment.

'What,' he mocked, his voice deep against her ear, 'are you going to walk all the way back to Winfields? Through the snow?' His arm clamped around her waist, bronzed fingers spreading against her taut, flat stomach. 'Be sensible, Sabrina Westlake.'

'How do you know my name?' she panted, her senses totally flustered. 'And how do you know I live at Winfields?' The warm, intimate contact with his body was both humiliating and alarming; if she had been a burglar alarm, she was sure, she would now be ringing hysterically. She swayed against the strength of his body as the mare set off in a gentle walk at his command, and clung to the arm around her waist. 'You *were* hunting me,' she said breathlessly. 'You knew I'd be riding in that field this morning.' She'd hardly had a chance to study that insolently handsome face properly, and she twisted round to face him, her cheeks pale. 'I think it's time you told me who you are, and what you want of me. Why do you say you're my enemy? I've never done anything to you. I've never even seen you in my life before last week!'

'Ah,' he smiled, 'but we have much in common.' His closeness brought the blood to her face again, and she turned away from his mocking, knowing eyes. 'You are beautiful, Sabrina,' he said, his voice as velvety as his smile. 'And beautifully-made.' She bit her lip as he drew her irresistibly closer against his own tough body. 'I think I am going to enjoy this game even more than I expected.'

'What game?' she demanded tensely, refusing to struggle against that scorching touch and give him the satisfaction of crushing her resistance.

'The game that you and I are playing,' he replied smoothly.

A raven screamed harshly overhead, and Sabrina shivered.

'I'm sorry,' she said frigidly, 'but I understand nothing. I'm not aware of having any connection with you at all.'

'That is something we shall soon remedy,' he said gently. 'But you are trembling, my dear Sabrina. Do I frighten you so much?'

'You don't frighten me at all,' she snapped.

'Then it must be my masculine charm,' he said mockingly. 'You are not very experienced in the ways of men, are you?'

'That's none of your damned business,' she retorted shakily. Thank God they were already on the cobbled road that led to Winfields, and she'd be able to escape from her extraordinary captor soon——

'Oh, but it is my business,' he cut through her thoughts silkily. 'It's all part of the game. Why is it, do you think,' he mused, 'that so beautiful a woman should be so shy of men? It's small wonder the newspapers have taken to calling you the Ice Maiden. Now I wonder, is your coldness some kind of psychological reaction to the fact that your father had so many affairs? Or did you just reject the idea of sharing all those millions with anybody else?'

'Let me go,' she spat, really angered by the taunt. '*Let me go!*' She struggled futilely against his iron-hard arm for a few seconds. Then, with dismissive casualness, he let her slide to the ground. She snatched Criterion's reins out of his hand, and glared up into the amused face with electric-blue eyes. 'I don't know who you are or what crazy game you think you're in,' she said, her voice tight with passion, 'but let me warn you right now that I'm not playing!'

'You have no choice,' he replied silkily, 'but to play my game. You will soon see the reason why.'

'If you come near me again,' she gritted, spots of colour burning in her beautiful, pale cheeks, 'I'll——'

'You will remember me,' he nodded. His face might have been carved from bronze now, all pretence of humour gone from the classical features. 'And we will meet again, Sabrina Westlake. Soon.'

'I don't know what you're talking about,' she said, shaking her head in disbelief. 'Who *are* you?'

'I shall repeat this one last time,' he said softly. The mockery in those grey eyes had become a terrifyingly icy contempt. 'I am your enemy, Sabrina Westlake.' God, she thought in quick fear, what have I done to this man to make him feel this way about me? The passion in his eyes melted back into sensual amusement as swiftly as it had appeared. 'You haven't far to walk now,' he said, pointing at the grim roofs of Winfields. 'Until we meet again, Sabrina.' With an ironic salute, he wheeled his horse round.

Numbly, she watched him go. The hooves of his horse struck sparks from the cobblestones as he broke into a gallop. He rode superbly, like some pagan half-man, an apparition from an ancient past. Then he was gone, hidden behind the dark birches. Only his hoofbeats trembled in the crisp air. The brief, electrifyingly tense encounter had left her shaking, almost stunned. A centaur, she thought dizzily. I've just met a centaur ... She patted Criterion's damp neck with a shaking hand. Had she stopped in the woods and eaten some weird toadstool? The crazily dramatic episode might almost have been an hallucination. But for Criterion's swollen fetlock.

She turned, and led the limping horse slowly towards the stables. He must have known she'd be out this morning, had probably hired his horse from the riding-school at Challenge Wood, cutting across the meadows between to intercept her on her own land. The calculating insolence of it set her anger flaring up again. Who in God's name is my enemy? The accent had been slightly foreign, but not unpleasantly so. French, perhaps? That only made the mystery deeper. Since her father's fatal stroke six months ago, her life had become so full of distortions and tensions that she hardly knew who were her friends and who her enemies any more. But then, she thought bitterly, when was it ever otherwise?

The memory of those piercing grey eyes haunted her as she found bandages in the stable, and bound up Criterion's leg. What had been in them? A disturbing mixture of contempt and sensuousness, of hatred and amusement.

This is a part of your heritage, too, she thought tiredly, isn't it, Daddy? The stallion stooped his beautiful head to hers, as though trying to console her. What lay at the bottom of this she had yet to find out; but she felt in her bones that it had something to do with Simon Westlake.

A memory of the whirr of sewing-machines and the companionable chatter at Phoenix rose sharp in her mind. A memory of the hope and simplicity of her student days. For three years she thought she'd escaped, become like everyone else.

Fool, she thought. Who were you trying to kid?

CHAPTER TWO

SABRINA arrived at Claridges five minutes late for her dinner with William on Thursday because of the weather, and he was already waiting for her at the alcove table she'd booked. He rose to meet her as she arrived.

'It's still snowing heavily,' she apologised. 'The traffic's barely crawling along.' She smiled at the old lawyer as they sat down. 'It's nice of you to make time for me like this, William.'

'It's my duty to keep you informed,' he said, watching her brush a few melting flakes of snow off her black gloves. She was wearing the sable coat over a simple black evening-dress and a plain string of matched pearls, and William's expression indicated approval. His eyes were touched with worry, though. 'Not that there's very much we can do, Sabrina. We can fight this bid, as Roderigo says—but I'm not sure whether we can ever win. It might be best to try and come to some kind of terms instead.'

'Well,' she replied, leaning back against the leather seat and pulling her coat open, 'at least you can tell me what options are likely to be open. You know that I'm completely inexperienced at all this.' She glanced up at the waiter who had materialised beside them. 'A dry sherry, please.'

'And a John Collins for me,' William ordered.

He looked back at Sabrina. 'Shall we wait for our drinks—or do you want to get down to business straight away?'

'There doesn't seem to be much time to waste,' she replied.

'There isn't,' he told her grimly. He slid a flat leather file towards her. 'I've made some notes for you to look through at your leisure, Sabrina. About the take-over bid.' He paused. 'And about everything else.'

She glanced at his face. 'You mean there's more than just the take-over bid?' she asked.

'A lot more,' he told her heavily. 'Do you know anything about Cressida?'

'Not really,' she confessed, covering her uneasiness with a smile. 'Are they big?'

'Very. They've got muscle. And that doesn't just mean money, I'm afraid. They have formidable technology behind them—and, as you'd expect from an Italian company, a genius for design. We're a long way behind them in almost everything we do. And over the last twelve months, Cressida have entered the section of the market that used to be your father's empire— radio, television and video components. There's no question that they've been deliberately trying to compete with Westlake. As though they wanted to shoulder us out of the market.'

'And are their products really that much better than ours?'

'Yes,' he said reluctantly. 'They're cheaper, they're more reliable—though I hate to admit it—and the design is better. They've been having a phenomenal success overseas. And now they're building up a brilliant distribution service here. In several major cities already, they can make the sale and deliver the goods before our trucks have even arrived at the outlet depots. We're losing some of our best customers.'

'Such as?'

'Woolworth's and John Lewis, for a start. And worse still, some of the biggest industrial buyers, too.'

'I see,' she said quietly. 'Is this as serious as it sounds, William?'

'Every bit,' the lawyer said simply. 'Westlake is being destroyed, Sabrina. Between the take-over bid in the market, and the ruthless competition from Cressida's factories, I'm very much afraid that we're going to the wall.'

'Are you telling me that Westlake is going bust?' Sabrina asked incredulously. It was as though a yawning hole had suddenly opened in front of her.

'You have to know the truth. And the truth is that we may do exactly that, very soon. If Cressida tightens her grip on our throats, we're going to die as a corporation.'

'But how can this have happened?' she asked, shaking her dark head. 'And how can it have happened so incredibly quickly, William?'

'I haven't a clue, my dear child. I don't know what our next move is. And I haven't the slightest damned idea why Cressida are doing this, either. It's like being stalked by some big beast of prey, Sabrina. It's almost as though they've got some spite, some vengeance to wreak on us.'

Ghostly fingers touched Sabrina's spine. 'My father made a lot of enemies,' she said, the familiar bitter twist pulling down the corners of her perfect mouth. 'Who runs Cressida?'

'A man called Leonardo l'Aquila.'

'That means The Eagle, doesn't it?' She tasted her sherry, her eyes unfocused. 'Perhaps Signor l'Aquila is intent on making some kind of point?'

'That's possible,' the lawyer agreed, sitting back in his seat and squeezing the bridge of his nose tiredly. 'I don't know.'

'What are we going to do, William?' she asked quietly.

'I've been trying to contact Cressida's lawyers for some days, Sabrina. Just for an informal meeting. Nothing. They're not interested. I don't mind telling you that Roderigo has been trying to contact l'Aquila at the same time—but he hasn't even had a glimpse of the man. All we get from his hotel is "not available at present".'

'You mean the man's in London?' she demanded.

'Yes.' He looked apologetic. 'You should have been told, I know, but Roderigo said——'

'Roderigo is not the head of this Corporation,' Sabrina said icily, suddenly angered at the way they'd kept all this from her. 'I am. And you should have told me about this *months* ago, William.'

'I know,' said the lawyer unhappily. 'But things have happend so damned fast, and . . .' He paused.

'And Roderigo forbade you to say anything to me about this crisis?' she supplied. William nodded slowly, sadly. She turned away, her blue eyes angry. Now was not the time for recriminations. 'William—be frank with me—how long has the Westlake Corporation got?'

'In time? That depends on how hard Cressida choose to push us. At the moment, we're teetering on the edge of the precipice. A fortnight or so away from disaster. One hard shove, and we could be in their pockets.'

'In *his* pockets,' she corrected drily.

He nodded his head. 'Westlake won't be worth a damn, Sabrina. Leonardo l'Aquila will have swallowed us whole.'

'A fortnight,' she repeated. 'And all those thousands of people who work for the Corporation, men with families, wives, mortgages——'

'Will be at the mercy of Cressida,' nodded the lawyer. 'Yes.'

'God help us, William.' She glanced up, and suddenly gasped aloud.

William leaned forward in alarm at the look on Sabrina's face. 'What is it?'

'That man,' she said sharply. Her eyes were riveted on the man at the next table. Her relentless pursuer, the man in the snow. The sight of him brought back the anger and confusion of Wednesday morning—and the fear. Beautifully dressed, he was apparently enjoying a quiet dinner alone. She hadn't noticed him until a second ago. He was sitting with negligent grace a few feet away, reading the *Financial Times* with his long legs comfortably crossed.

'Well, well,' William said in grim surprise. 'I didn't see him—he must have just arrived.'

'You know him?' she enquired, not taking her eyes off the tanned face.

'Yes. And so will you, before long.' William's voice was grave. 'That's Leo l'Aquila. The man behind Cressida Industrial.'

'That man owns Cressida?' She glanced swiftly at William. 'Are you *sure*?'

'No doubt about it. He spends most of his time in Italy, and very few people know who he is here; He must have come to London to supervise the take-over.'

'God!' Sabrina looked back at l'Aquila. He seemed casually absorbed in his paper, yet her instincts told her he was one hundred per cent aware of their consternation. And one hundred per cent amused. So *that* was what his frightening pursuit of her had been all about! The contemptuous triumph of a man about to conquer.

Instinctively, she pulled her coat around her, trying to shake off the chill of fear that had struck at her, and stood up.

'What are you doing?' William asked.

'I'm going to speak to him,' she replied quietly. She was damned if she was going to let herself be mocked and intimidated by any man, no matter how powerful. His presence here tonight was no more an accident than the last two times. Well, Sabrina Westlake was tired of playing games! 'Excuse me, William.'

She walked across to the other table, her eyes cold as blue ice. He looked up calmly as she approached.

'Signor l'Aquila, I presume,' she said frigidly. 'I don't think I need to introduce myself, do I? My lawyer tells me that you're trying to buy my company.'

Leonardo l'Aquila turned the pale-pink newspaper on the tablecloth so that she could see the stock exchange listings. 'Westlake shares have dropped another twelve points,' he said by way of reply. 'It has become scarcely worth buying them, really.' The glint of cruel amusement which had haunted her for a week now reappeared momentarily in his eyes as he stood up and surveyed her with calm interest.

She'd folded the high collar of the sable around her cheeks and mouth, and from the vantage point of this dark fortress, her deep blue eyes looked back at him with ill-concealed anger. He was taller than she had remembered, and that suggestion of tense power about him was both magnetic and threatening from close by. Once again, he was impeccably dressed, in a black evening jacket and a black bow tie.

He reached out, and gently but firmly folded back the sable collar which she was clutching around her face. A glint appeared in the grey eyes as the perfect oval of her face was framed against the midnight sheen of the fur. 'So you've found out who I am. This is an unexpected pleasure.'

'Rubbish,' Sabrina snapped. 'You knew I was going to be here, just as you did the last two times. Why are you following me around?'

'Surely,' he murmured, 'you're a bit paranoid?' For an instant she stared into his eyes, trying to fathom the strange expression there—mockery? Dislike? And then she broke the spell, stepping away from him and sitting at his table without invitation.

'Let's not waste time with small-talk, Signor l'Aquila,' she said tersely, her deep voice shaking more than she cared to acknowledge. 'You had some reason for coming here tonight. If it was to intimidate me, I should warn you that I don't frighten easily.'

'No?' he replied coolly. He sat down, lacing his fingers together. 'Then you are indeed Simon Westlake's daughter. Nothing frightened him, either. Did it?'

There was a sneer somewhere in the remark, and Sabrina felt the flush come to her cheeks. 'I'm not responsible for my father's behaviour,' she said tersely.

'No? Don't they say that the sins of the fathers shall be visited on the children?'

'If they say that, they're cruel and vindictive,' she retorted.

'It's beside the point,' he shrugged. 'You are responsible for his company, now. You *are* Westlake.' He poured her a glass of wine from the bottle at his elbow. 'You've been titular head of the Corporation for—how long? Six months?'

'Shorter than that,' she corrected. Despite this man's intimidating presence, she had an extraordinary feeling of having known him a long time already, and she tried hard to shake off the slightly hypnotised feeling in her head. 'That's neither here nor there. What I want to know——'

'Five, then,' he interrupted. 'And do you

intend to maintain Westlake's high standards of
. . .' He paused drily. 'Business morals?'

'I intend to run the Corporation in the best way
possible,' she retorted angrily.

'Ah. So you *do* intend to run it?'

'What do you mean?' she asked, uneasy.

'Rumour has it that you're going to hand the
reins over to the esteemed Roderigo Gomez,' he
replied, watching her with piercing grey eyes. 'I
take it that's untrue?'

'You can take nothing.' She caught William's
worried gaze over Signor l'Aquila's shoulder,
and drew a deep breath, trying to control her
anger. 'I don't want to talk about myself. I
want to talk about your take-over bid for
Westlake.'

'Haven't you just told me that you *are*
Westlake?' he asked mildly. 'Besides which, I
haven't made any bid for your corporation.'

'But you intend to. You've been attacking the
Westlake Corporation for months.'

'Are you offering to sell?' he asked with
deceptive mildness.

'Certainly not!' she snapped.

'Spoken like a true daughter of Simon
Westlake,' he purred.

'So you can give up any idea of taking Westlake
over,' she went on, ignoring the taunt, 'because
it's not for sale.'

'Very well, Ice Maiden.' He toasted her
mockingly. 'If you think that merely saying so
makes you safe—then Westlake is not for sale.'
He drank, then met her eyes with shocking
directness. 'Do not forget, though, when you go

to sleep in your ice palace tonight, that what a man cannot buy he may decide . . . to take.'

She knew in that second that he wasn't just talking about Westlake. He was talking about *her*. Arrogant, vile man! She stood up, pulling her fur around her.

'I'm not staying to bandy words with you,' she said in a low, shaky voice.

'Then, once more—until we meet again, Sabrina.' She turned away from the coolly insulting smile, and walked swiftly back to William.

'What is it?' he asked worriedly, rising to meet her.

'The cold-blooded *bastard*,' she muttered, more to herself than William. The lawyer's eyebrows shot up at her unladylike language.

'Has he said something to you——?'

'Just that he wants Westlake,' she said explosively.

'In so many words?'

'By implication.' He'd finished paying his bill, and she watched him with clenched teeth as he walked out. He didn't spare either of them a backward glance. 'He's not going to get it, William,' she vowed, her eyes narrowed to sapphire slits, 'I'll stop him if it's the last thing I do! Tell me how we're going to do it.'

'I have already discussed the outline of our plan of resistance with Miss Westlake,' William told the impassive Board. 'Though I must say here and now that the threat is a great deal more serious than the Board seems to believe.' There were a few smiles, and Roderigo Gomez's impatient sigh made it obvious that he thought William's concern about Cressida slightly hysterical.

Sabrina had been sitting cool and silent during the first long hour of the board-meeting, seemingly untouched by the cigar-smoke or the highly technical talk that rapidly filled the room. The masculine setting made her beauty all the more exotic. The lustrous wave of her hair, as iridescently glossy as a raven's wing, set off her creamy skin strikingly. Her mouth, perfect and leaf-shaped, neither smiled nor relaxed into boredom as she listened to the arguments of the eight powerful men gathered there.

Only once did she let her eyes stray to the portrait in oils that dominated the boardroom. For a moment her gaze met the implacable stare of the man who had been her father. *Father*, she thought bitterly. I never even called you that. Though I could find many names for you.

To the world he'd been a heroic villain, the man everyone loved to hate. The man who'd built a financial empire with his cunning and bare will, devouring or crushing all who stood in his way. To Sabrina and her mother, he'd been nemesis. A cruel, inescapable destiny. You killed my mother, she told the fierce blue eyes silently, but you won't kill me.

He'd been one of those men who are born to make their way in the world over the dead bodies of others. Marrying a gentle, helpless heiress had been a quick way of raising the capital he needed to start making his dreams come true. There had been no place in such a man's life for tenderness. Her father had needed the kind of women he could devour and discard, women who'd be satisfied with money. Not a wife and babe who'd needed love.

Listening abstractedly to the discussion about the Cressida bid, she thought of the way her mother had faded into a white-haired ghost. The way she'd died, less than five years ago, just another of her father's victims. *And just when I thought I'd escaped to my own life, you had to go and die. And loop the noose of your empire round my neck.*

What a pity you aren't alive now, she thought suddenly. You'd have found an adversary worthy of you at last. She remembered the ruthless self-confidence of Leo l'Aquila, the thrusting yet subtle aggression of his personality. Yes, the Eagle would make her father a fitting opponent . . .

A general shuffling of minute-notes dragged her attention back to Roderigo.

'We are agreed, then,' he was saying, 'on our policy for fighting off the so-called Cressida bid. The owner's concern has been noted.' The scornful glance he shot William Cattermole made it abundantly clear that he resented his influence with Sabrina. 'Cattermole will take charge, and will report back to this board if any change takes place. I have every confidence that we can counter any moves this foreign firm might conceivably make.' There was a chorus of 'Hear, hears' from around the table. 'Which brings us,' he went on, 'to the question of the components factory on Tyneside.' Sabrina shifted slightly in her chair, her senses now fully alert on what was going on. 'I don't think I need to go into great detail,' he said smoothly, his hooded eyes probing the faces around the mahogany table. 'It's a simple question of trimming off some of the Corporation's excess fat. This plant has barely broken even for the past three years. Over the past half-year, it's actually made a loss of two hundred and five thousand pounds. At the beginning of the year there was a long industrial stoppage over wages which halted production for six weeks, and following that, a fire destroyed part of the works. There's also the question of machinery. Much of the plant is now obsolete, and needs replacing, at an estimated cost of around half a million.'

Roderigo's aquiline, sallow face nodded over the sheaf of papers he held in one hand. 'You've all seen these calculations. We can make up what the Tyneside factory produces by increasing production at six other Westlake plants in Wales and the Midlands. That will enable us to close down the Tyneside plant by the end of the year. The site and the buildings are a prime industrial estate, and should fetch an excellent price. Even the machinery will probably be saleable. On top of that, nine hundred men who are presently rather less than productive will be removed from the Westlake payroll, a saving of something like eighty thousand pounds a year.' He leaned back in his chair, lighting a cigarillo. 'Any questions?'

Sabrina watched the directors with alert blue eyes. There was a vague murmur around the table, but before anyone voiced any opinion, Roderigo nodded briskly.

'Excellent. Then I move that we take an immediate vote on the closure. Those in favour of closing, please raise your hands——'

Sabrina drew a deep breath. 'Just a moment, please.' Eight faces turned in surprise at the sound of her cool voice. Give me strength, she prayed urgently, and tried to keep her faint smile relaxed. 'Before we decide to put nine hundred men out of work, shouldn't we at least discuss it?'

'I had no idea you had any opinions on the subject, Sabrina,' Roderigo said, his brown eyes cold. 'The floor is all yours, of course.' William Cattermole was watching her with intelligent, interested eyes. She laced her fingers, still smiling.

'Well,' she said gently, moving into a speech she'd been thinking about all week, 'the first thing that occurs to me is that it's not exactly moral to put nearly a thousand men out of work in an area which has traditionally had very high unemployment. Many of those men have families who depend upon them. Most of them are over forty, and their chances of finding another job— ever—are slim.'

'Granted,' Roderigo said with a shrug. 'It's tough on them. But we can't sustain a loss for ever. As for what you call "morality", it has nothing to do with business, Sabrina. Morality doesn't bring in profits.'

'A statement worthy of my father,' she said with quiet irony. The directors' eyes were riveted on her, and she glanced round their faces, hoping they couldn't see how badly she was shaking inside. 'But isn't closing the factory down a rather drastic solution to a simple problem?'

'A two-hundred-thousand-pound loss isn't exactly a simple problem,' one of the other directors said shortly. 'It's a haemorrhage!' She met his hostile eyes without flinching, remembering the way he'd tried to patronise her when she'd first inherited the Corporation.

'If you'll pardon me, Mr Lombard,' she answered, 'that's rather a dramatic statement coming from a man who claims a company car costing well over fifty thousand pounds.' Lombard's face purpled as a general shuffling of interest stirred the other directors. 'Not to mention,' she went on smoothly, 'the cost of your chauffeur.' She looked around the table with clear eyes. 'Let's not kid ourselves that two or three thousand pounds here or there is going to break Westlake. This Board of Directors spends almost half a million pounds a year on itself. Not on the firm. Not on the employees. On itself. Half a *million*!' She ticked the points off on her fingers. 'Company cars—including our three Rolls Royces. Bloated expense-accounts, stuffed with ridiculous dodges that even a child could see through.' There were some embarrassed smiles round the table, and a sharp nod from William. 'Entertainment allowances. Unspecified slush funds. Thousands of pounds worth of unnecessary office furniture. Unnecessary trips abroad—with secretaries. Misuse of petty cash funds. The list goes on and on.' She swung in her chair to face

Roderigo's furious eyes. 'In the face of *that*, Mr Chairman, the loss of nine hundred jobs isn't just immoral. It's criminal.'

'Sabrina,' he said thickly, his sallow face mottled. 'We're making allowances for your position and your ignorance of the way a sophisticated business operates.' He ground his cigarillo out. 'This is neither the time nor the place to start criticising the Board's spending—'

'Pardon me,' she interrupted, her voice calm. 'We are not discussing the Board. We are discussing the closure of a factory. I simply wanted to point out that if there's any fat to be trimmed off the Westlake Corporation, there are better places to begin than with nine hundred working men.'

Geoffrey Lawrence, one of the youngest directors, leaned forward, his expression interested. 'What are you suggesting, then, Miss Westlake?'

'I'm suggesting that the Tyneside plant needn't be scrapped,' she said, feeling that she was making one convert at least—two, if William Cattermole's expression signified approval. 'The factory hasn't been productive, granted. But then, on the Chairman's admission, the equipment is outmoded, and there's been a destructive fire.' She glanced from Geoffrey Lawrence to Roderigo. 'As for the strike—well, I've gone into the figures, and it seems to me that those men were definitely underpaid.'

'You seem to have been doing your homework,' Roderigo said, the sneer in his voice barely disguised. 'But if you'll forgive me for interrupting, Sabrina, you really aren't qualified to judge on such matters.' He smiled, his face vulturine. 'I understand that you're tempted to see problems like this as being very simple, but they're not.'

'Oh?' She bit back her anger at the insulting tone of his voice. 'Isn't it true that if we were to invest the half-million that this factory needs, it would be productive again within a year? And if we put the problem to the men, wouldn't they give us a guarantee to raise output, rather than face closure?'

The murmur of agreement that went round the table only seemed to infuriate Roderigo Gomez more, and Sabrina saw his wrinkled fingers grasp the edge of the table convulsively.

'Sabrina,' he said heavily, his expression ugly, 'I've already had to say this once this morning—but you are *not* qualified to judge on matters of company policy.'

Sabrina sat very still. 'And I've had to remind *you* once already,' she said quietly, 'that I am the owner of this Corporation, Roderigo.' There was a tense silence that strained her already stretched nerves unbearably. But she held his gaze without blinking.

'Are you trying to force a confrontation with me?' Roderigo hissed, as though there were no one else in the room.

'No,' she replied, her stomach aching with nerves. 'I'm trying to save almost a thousand jobs.'

'You're being childish,' he spat. 'The Westlake Corporation isn't a dress-shop, Sabrina! And that factory is a useless asset!'

'You've just said that it's a prime industrial site,' she retorted. 'It's been badly managed for three years now, and relations between the staff and the management have been allowed to deteriorate to a disgraceful extent. My experience may be limited to a small design studio, but even I know that with good-will and co-operation, *anything* can be achieved.' She took a breath to calm herself. 'In my opinion, that factory could be working at full capacity in one year. In two, it could be bringing in the highest profits. But it needs to be modernised, and the local management need to be shaken up.' Forcing herself to relax her rigid muscles, she turned to the rest of the Board, who were staring at her with frozen expressions. 'My father made this Corporation powerful by trampling over other people. But he's dead now. And that way of doing things also died with him.' Warmed by William's steady nod of approval, she went on, the words she was saying coming from her very heart of hearts. 'Westlake can no longer afford to smash its way through any obstacle, the way that it used to do. It's time this firm started taking some social responsibility for the people who work for it. And if we treat them right,' she said emphatically, 'I know they'll treat us right. That doesn't mean just a happier workforce and a better public image—it means better productivity, higher efficiency, more profits.' She stopped, realising that she had just made her longest speech ever, and feeling that her nerves were just about to give way out of sheer exhaustion. 'That's all I wanted to say.'

'In which case,' Geoffrey Lawrence said unexpectedly, 'I propose we get back to that vote on closure right now. Mr Chairman?'

Roderigo's wrinkled face was grey with anger, but he forced a smile. 'One last thing, if you please,' he said in a gravelly voice. 'We all respect the owner's sentiments. I regret that they happen to be at odds with my own judgment on this occasion.' Sabrina inclined her head, not trusting herself to speak. 'May I remind the Board that Miss Westlake has been the owner of this Corporation for six months. I have been Vice-Chairman, under Simon Westlake, for nineteen years.' His glare round the table made it clear how he expected his audience to react. 'Now. All those in favour of closure, please indicate.' In a complete silence, Sabrina looked around the table. Two hands were raised—Roderigo's and the purple-faced director's. Roderigo's voice was quivering with anger as he went on, 'Those in favour of keeping the factory open?' Six hands went up. Numbly, Sabrina raised her own. Roderigo's eyes were like stones as they met hers. 'Motion defeated,' he said softly. There were smiles all round the table as a buzz of talk went up. The purple-faced director was looking as though he now rather wished he'd voted the other way. Relief swept over Sabrina as she nodded to William's smile of approval. The jobs had been saved. And more than that, she'd spoken her mind to the Board of Directors, and maybe set Westlake on a completely new course.

But she had to realise as she leaned forward to hear Geoffrey Lawrence's congratulations that

Roderigo now knew to what extent she was prepared to fight to stop her father's methods from continuing in the Corporation. It was his choice now—whether to fight, or admit that the old law of ruthless exploitation was now dead and gone.

Slowly, she allowed her nervous muscles to relax. The Westlake Corporation was an appalling burden round her neck. But before she could even think of freeing herself from it, she had to be sure that she wasn't going to be delivering all the lives that depended upon it into the hands of an even greater tyranny than her father's.

Five days later, the letter arrived. It was with her other mail on the tray Mrs Beeston brought to her at breakfast. She always had breakfast in the plant-filled conservatory, overlooking the formal garden to the rear of the house. She loved its peace and tranquillity.

She slit the embossed envelope open absently, and studied the card inside with widening eyes.

21 February

My Dear Miss Westlake,
By now you will have realised that there are matters of mutual financial interest which must be discussed soon. I will speak to no Westlake representative except you. Alone. I suggest dinner this Thursday night. My car will call for you at Winfields. 6:30 p.m.

l'Aquila.

My car will call for you. The arrogance of the letter that had arrived that morning had almost taken her breath away. Who in heaven's name did he think he was? The strong black writing was like the man, imperious, dominant. Sabrina gulped down her coffee, and reached for the telephone. The man she wanted to talk to was William Cattermole.

'I've had a summons,' she informed him acidly. 'Listen to this.' She read him the note. 'Sounds like an imperial command, doesn't it? What do you think of it?'

'I think this is it,' William said in a quiet voice. 'He's going to make you an offer. God, I'd give anything to be with you on Thursday.'

'Then you think I ought to go?' Sabrina said, slightly disappointed. She'd been planning to give l'Aquila a monumental snub.

'There's no question,' William said urgently. 'You *must* talk to him, Sabrina. There just isn't any time any more.'

'You sound as if you've had bad news,' she probed, feeling uneasy.

'The worst. Cressida are about to launch their most powerful onslaught yet. They've just announced it.' He drew a breath, sounding shaky. 'It's called Tristar. A new range of components, covering every field that Westlake are in—radio, television, lighting, home electrical, recording, *everything*. In a month's time Tristar will start hitting the major outlets in the U.K. The range has already been a brilliant success in Europe and the Far East. Here, it's going to blow Westlake right off the map.'

'Can't we compete . . .?'

'Not a hope. The technology is light-years

ahead of ours. Their product is cheaper, better, more reliable. It's our death-knell, Sabrina.'

'Are you *sure* you aren't exaggerating?' Sabrina asked in disbelief. 'It sounds almost incredible, William.'

'The only incredible thing,' he retorted with uncharacteristic violence, 'is the refusal of responsible people at Westlake to take Cressida seriously! Listen to me—if you don't want to see your own fortune ruined and your company obliterated, you've got to listen to what l'Aquila says. For God's sake, though, don't agree to anything until you've consulted the Board. Or at least me.'

'Yes, of course,' she said tiredly. The conservatory had suddenly become oppressively humid. 'And of course I'll go.'

Once again, she didn't have any choice, did she?

She stood, pale and self-contained in front of the full-length mirror on Thursday evening, a strangely dark figure in the white bedroom. Almost the only touches of colour about her were the deep blue of her eyes, the scarlet of her lovely mouth. The diamond, one of her father's last gifts to her, glittered icily at her throat.

'You look like a dream, ma'am,' Mrs Beeston breathed, coming in with her sable. But the expression on her face was more awe-struck than admiring. Sabrina turned to her with a set smile.

'Thank you.' She was wearing one of the dresses she had designed and made herself out of a priceless velvet of such a deep red as to be almost black. Only where the light struck its hidden shimmers did the deep red glow. The neckline plunged extravagantly deep. Across her left shoulder a silver dragon snarled, and from the severely close-fitting waist, the dress followed the line of her hips and thighs, showing off her figure with an insolent confidence. From her immaculate court shoes to the iridescent blackness of her hair, she was a figure of formidable, magnificent beauty.

She had just pulled on the sable coat, a sombre token of her first meeting with Leonardo l'Aquila; and the rest of her ensemble was scarcely less sombre.

'I've never seen you looking like that,' Mrs Beeston said, slightly nervously. 'You look like a queen. But just a little frightening, too.'

'Good,' Sabrina said grimly, shrugging on the fur coat. 'I'm going to meet a rather frightening man. Don't wait up for me, Mrs Beeston. I may be late.'

The big drawing-room was lit only by a small table-lamp, and in the dim light, she poured herself a sherry, suddenly feeling the need for something to sustain her courage, and went to the wide bay-window. The world outside was dark, wintry and forbidding. She could barely see the gleam of snow on the ground, and could only guess at the bare fields and stark trees that lay across that dark landscape. Her landscape. If Leonardo l'Aquila chose to leave it for her.

And somewhere out in that darkness, Criterion, her big bay stallion, slept in his warm stall. How she would have loved to be able to run out into that wintry darkness, to have led the big horse

out into the night, to have hoisted up her dress
and ridden him, bare-legged, across the snow—to
feel the icy wind on her breast, the pounding
power of the horse beneath her, the speed and
thrill of a night gallop! And to have ridden him,
hard and fast, into the wild wood, and there to
have slipped off, panting, and to have lain in the
snow, catching her breath, with no companion
but the pale moon!

'Miss Westlake?'

She turned slowly. The dumpy figure of Mrs
Beeston was silhouetted in the doorway.

'Yes, Mrs Beeston?'

'The chauffeur is here, ma'am.'

She nodded, then put the sherry-glass down
with a tiny sigh.

'Thank you,' she said with a smile that did not
waver. 'Tell him I'm coming now.'

She pulled the dark comfort of the sable
around her shoulders, and walked out. The
chauffeur who was waiting for her bowed silently
before escorting her to the gleaming Silver Spirit
that stood on the gravelled driveway. The
interior of the magnificent car was leather-
scented and opulent—and cold. As cold as
charity. She leaned forward to ask the chauffeur
to put on the heater, and he complied without a
word. As silent as its driver, the big car nosed out
of the tall wrought-iron gates that led into the
quiet country road which in its turn led on to the
M4. And London.

CHAPTER THREE

SABRINA stepped on to the pavement amid a light sprinkling of snow. They had driven through a maze of streets which she no longer recognised. The restaurant in front of which the chauffeur had halted was called The Dragon Pearl, and its ornate, authentic Chinese façade was hung with lanterns which glowed and flickered in the falling flakes. The chauffeur held open the door, and she entered the softly-lit anteroom beyond.

A young Chinese girl was waiting.

'May I take your coat, Miss Westlake?' she asked in her soft voice. Surprised to be greeted by name, Sabrina glanced down at the exquisite, lotus-blossom face and almond eyes, and shook her head.

'Not yet, thank you. I'm still cold.'

The girl bowed and led her through the arched doorway at the other end of the room. Sabrina had no time to examine the beautiful hangings on the walls, nor the intricately-carved wooden furniture, both of which she was sure were genuine and priceless antiques from some long-forgotten Peking palace. But clearly, this was no ordinary restaurant!

The room beyond was more austere than the first, and lit with a soft light that made it mysterious, despite the simplicity of its colourings. At the far end of the room, a brazier filled the air with a soft cloud of aromatic incense, and another tall screen partitioned a part of this room off, too.

He was waiting for her there, tall and dark and immaculately dressed as ever.

His eyes rested on her with smouldering pleasure. 'My dear Sabrina,' he murmured, 'you are quite dazzling.'

'Let's not waste time with compliments, Signor l'Aquila,' she said tersely, her body rigid with tension. 'You summoned me here to discuss what you called matters of mutual financial interest. Shall we get on with it?'

'Nothing comes before business with the Westlakes, does it?' he said gently. She shook her head, her mouth set with anger.

'You're smashing my company, Signor l'Aquila. Thousands of my employees stand to lose their jobs through you. I don't wish to discuss social niceties with you.'

'Mei-Ling.' He turned away with complete indifference in the midst of her outburst. The Chinese girl, whose calm, golden face gave no sign that she had overheard any of Sabrina's angry words, appeared as if by magic. Leonard. l'Aquila nodded at Sabrina. 'Take Miss Westlake's coat, if you please.'

'I don't——' Suddenly conscious that by losing her temper she was giving him the advantage, Sabrina stopped herself and shrugged the heavy fur into the girl's waiting arms. Uncomfortably, she felt as though she were shedding a suit of armour in front of a deadly adversary—and her insecurity was confirmed as she saw Leonardo l'Aquila's eyes drop with insolent flattery to her breasts and the curve of her hips under the wine-red velvet.

'Shall we eat?' Unwillingly, she let him take her arm. The muscles of his body were as hard as steel under the perfect fit of his clothes, and she tried to suppress a shudder at their touch. He felt her involuntary movement, and looked down at her with amused grey eyes as he led her behind the screen, and through the doorway beyond.

'Are you scared of me, Sabrina?'

'I would prefer to be called Miss Westlake,' she snapped. 'And of course you don't scare me!'

'No? That is a pleasure yet to come, then,' he smiled. And there was something in his smile which spoke of a cruel and ruthless triumph.

They passed under the bamboo curtain into the dining-room, and she wondered whether Leonardo l'Aquila could feel just exactly how scared of him she really was.

A pale, mother-of-pearl light suffused the next room. The floor, she noticed, was laid with beautifully-shaped Burmese teak tiles. Only one table had been laid in the small, octagonal room, and only one other person was in it—a middle-aged Chinese woman who did not look up from her instrument as they walked in. She was playing softly and reclining on a cushion some distance from the low table which had been set out with antique *famille verte* bowls, chopsticks, and a vase of chrysanthemums and hibiscus flowers. The calm simplicity of the room, though, was deceptive; and as she sat down on the low, comfortable seat, Sabrina noticed that the furniture in the room—chairs, couches, and small occasional tables, was exquisite—the same ornate, ancient pattern as the things she had noticed in the foyer. And the silk paintings all around them were exquisite, too, classically beautiful in a way that she had seldom seen in Britain. This was not the tawdry pseudo-Chinese paraphernalia which was all most Europeans knew—this was the delicate, perfect rose of classical Chinese taste.

'Do you approve?' he asked, watching her with unfathomable eyes as they sat down.

'It's very beautiful,' she said stiffly. 'I had no idea that this place existed.'

'I thought the simplicity of the surroundings would be conducive to talk,' he nodded. 'I've taken the liberty of ordering the meal in advance, so we shall not be bothered with waiters or menus. Mei-Ling will simply bring each dish through when we wish it. Are you hungry?'

'No,' she said coldly, and made a mental vow that she would leave her food utterly untasted tonight, as a snub to this arrogant man. She judged him to be between thirty-two and thirty-five. That he was devastatingly handsome was becoming more and more obvious as she considered his face through her lowered lashes. There was a commanding power about him that she recognised as coming from success and wealth—not inherited wealth, but the power which had been siezed and won personally. His hands were indicative of his personality, she thought—beautiful and elegant, they were also formidably strong. His voice was like velvet, slightly and pleasantly accented; a voice that would have seduced hundreds of beautiful women, she thought bitterly.

'Shall we start with a glass of this excellent Reisling?' he suggested. She shook her head.

'I'd prefer a glass of Perrier water,' she answered coolly. He smiled as he lifted the bottle from its bucket.

'I think wine would be more appropriate,' he said with calm indifference. She tried to snatch her glass away, but he took it firmly, filled it with the pale-gold wine, and passed it back to her. This tiny confrontation infuriated her unreasonably, and her hand was shaking as she set the glass down.

'A toast,' he said in his deep purr. 'The Westlake Corporation.'

She did not touch her glass as he drank. Apparently unmoved, he took her bowl, and helped her to some of the dark green biscuit-like delicacies on the beautiful old lacquer tray.

'This is made from dried seaweed,' he informed her, his grey eyes meeting hers with a hint of amusement. 'An unpromising beginning— but go on, try it.'

Unwillingly, she lifted one of the light biscuits to her mouth. It was surprisingly delicious, crisp and salty.

'How is Señor Gomez, your esteemed Chairman?' he went on politely. 'I believe he has been trying to contact me for some days—but I have been so busy.' He smiled a leopard's mocking smile. 'You know how it is.'

'Yes,' she said quietly. 'It must be hard work destroying a Corporation, Signor l'Aquila.'

The full, passionate mouth smiled in deprecation.

'Destroying? No. Merely competing, my dear Sabrina.'

'But why do you have to compete?' she asked, her voice taut. 'Why do you hate Westlake so much?'

'Do try your wine—it is delicious.'

'So you're not going to answer.' She stared at him, wondering what lay at the heart of this enigmatic, complicated man. With a mental shrug, she picked up her glass, and drank. The wine was cool and tasted of all the wild flowers of a French summer.

'Better than water?' he enquired.

'It's superb, and you know it,' she acknowledged, and glanced around the beautiful room, at the lute-player, whose plangent melody was drifting peacefully through the air. Whatever else he was, he had style. 'I presume you're accustomed to the best in everything, Signor?'

'I'd be jaded indeed if I were accustomed to the best,' he smiled. 'Shall we say I have a taste for it.' He clapped his hands lightly, and at once the young Chinese girl came in through the arched doorway, carrying a long tray of small bowls, which she laid on the table between them. A sizzling assortment of delicious smells assailed Sabrina; each bowl contained some delicate dish, a selection so varied in colour, smell, and appearance, that she was bewildered.

'Let me help you.' He leaned forward, and picked something from a selection of the bowls to put on her plate. 'The essence of classical

Chinese cooking,' he went on, 'is contrast. Sweet and sour, bitter and plain, hot and cold, dry and moist. The Chinese are very civilised people, don't you think? They don't bother with the ritualised distinction which characterises, say, French cooking. Here, one simply helps oneself, mixing and contrasting at one's pleasure.' He passed the plate back to her, and she surveyed the tantalizing plateful with frustration.

'Is something the matter?' he enquired gently. She looked up at him with resentful eyes.

'I don't know how to use chopsticks,' she said shortly. 'Can't I have a knife and fork?'

'I don't know whether Mei-Ling's father possesses such barbarous implements,' he said mildly.

She was forced to smile. 'Then I'm going to have a very hungry evening.'

'Let me show you—it's not difficult.'

He took her hand, tucking one of the chopsticks into the vee of her thumb-joint. 'Hold that one firmly,' he commanded, 'and use the other so—as though it were a pencil.' The touch of his fingers was warm against her cool hands, and for some reason the contact raised gooseflesh all over her body. Feeling the blood rushing to her pale cheeks, she wrestled with the uncomfortable implements. His laugh was soft—she felt, rather than heard it—and the colour stayed bright in her cheeks. Beneath the formidable exterior of the man there was a bewitching charm, utterly male yet somehow warm.

'Not like that. Like this.' Deftly, he lifted a crisp morsel off his plate and held it to her lips.

After a second's hesitation at the intimacy of the gesture, she opened her mouth and he popped it in. Her eyes widened in appreciation at the delicious taste. 'You see the rewards of dexterity?' he smiled. 'Try again.'

She managed to lift a few flakes of pork this time, and got them to her mouth without spillage.

'Better?' she asked defiantly.

'Much. Don't let me down too badly—Mei-Ling thinks I'm quite civilised for a Westerner.'

'You come to London often, then?' Sabrina probed.

'I like mixing my cities. London, Florence, Paris—each city has its own charm, no?' His eyes were bright. 'Even Manchester, perhaps.'

'You know a lot about me,' she said wryly. She ate another mouthful before going on. Subtle, delicate, fiery or sweet, the flavours vied with one another for attention, yet the overall effect was deliciously harmonious. Yes—it was above all a deeply civilised meal. 'Manchester is a great city,' she went on, 'but not a beautiful one.' She managed to secure a prawn, and chewed it appreciatively. 'I went to university there until I was twenty, and made a lot of friends there. That's why I settled there and started the design shop when I graduated. There was no reason for me to come to London.'

'You didn't see much of your father, then?' he asked casually.

'We didn't exactly get on,' she said tersely. Mention of her father had reminded her that this was not a pleasant evening with a stunningly handsome man, but a grim battle of wills. 'Which brings us back to the Westlake Corporation, Signor l'Aquila.'

'My name is Leo,' he said, smiling gently. 'You won't compromise your integrity by using it.'

'About Westlake,' she pressed, refusing to be put off. 'You're obviously a cultured man, probably a very wealthy one already.' He merely smiled, not acknowledging the hinted question. 'Is there no way you can be persuaded away from destroying my Corporation?'

'*Your* Corporation,' he repeated, as though testing her.

'I never wanted it, Signor. But by attacking it, you force me to defend it.'

'You haven't chosen an easy task, then.' He dabbed at his lips with his napkin, and sat back. 'Things look very bad for your Corporation, Ice Maiden.'

'Thanks to you,' she rejoined cuttingly.

'Your shares have dropped to an all-time low,' he continued, ignoring her interruption. 'The stock will soon be almost worthless. Your order-books are nearly empty. Westlake products are no longer selling. What's more,' he added, toying with his wine glass, studying the amber liquor against the light, 'your finances are badly over-extended. Your esteemed father borrowed a great deal of money from the merchant banks to finance his change-over three years ago. Did you know that?'

'Yes, but——'

'Then you also know that these debts still stand. And unless Westlake can meet the repayments in less than a year's time ...' He smiled, letting the silence complete his sentence.

'You seem very well-informed about Westlake,' she said tightly. So much for his veneer of charm!

'Oh yes. I'm very well-informed about Westlake. You find yourself in grave difficulties, I'm afraid,' he said, his expression parodying sympathy. 'I wonder how I can help?'

'I'll bet you lie awake worrying about it,' she said acidly. And she'd just started to like the man! 'Please spare me your irony, Signor.'

'Very well. But there is another matter which has contributed to Westlake's predicament.' He reached into his breast pocket, took out a folded sheet of paper, and tossed it on to the table in front of her.

'What does it say?' she asked, not looking at it.

'Your Señor Gomez has been robbing you blind for months, Sabrina.'

'What do you mean?' she demanded angrily.

'I mean exactly what I say. You have been blind, and he has been robbing you.' He nodded a little grimly. 'I should not have had my success against Westlake quite so soon but for his unwitting co-operation. Gomez has been siphoning off Westlake's profits at the rate of sixty to a hundred-thousand pounds a month.'

'You're lying!' she accused, the colour fading from her cheeks. 'It's impossible!'

'Most of the money, of course, is in his private account in Mexico City. Indeed, within a very few days, I expect to hear that Señor Gomez himself is also in Mexico City—the first, fattest, cleverest rat to abandon the sinking ship.'

She gaped at him for a few seconds, then snatched up the piece of paper, and scanned it with disbelieving blue eyes.

'I don't quite understand this,' she said, her voice shaking, 'but it's private material from Westlake's computer system. How did you get hold of it?'

'It's a list of payments,' he said, ignoring her question. 'It details the amounts Gomez has stolen from Westlake, Sabrina. From you. His speciality, as you will see, is selling off "unprofitable" parts of the company. Such as the firm on Tyneside you were defending so manfully the other day.' Once again, the cruel smile was back in his eyes. 'It seems there is not much honour among thieves.'

'My God.' She thought back to Roderigo's almost unreasoning anger about her opposition on Friday. Could that really be why he'd wanted to sell off the plant? So that he could pocket the proceeds himself? 'But—but how could he have got away with it?' she asked breathlessly.

He shrugged indifferently. 'He didn't intend the deception to last long. Just long enough to build up a handsome nest-egg before he left the country. Perhaps some of the other board-members have been conniving with him. I haven't bothered to find out. If you want more evidence of your Chairman's criminal dealings, I can get my accountants to supply them.'

'Who are you?' she asked shakily, 'some kind of avenging angel?'

'That is not a bad description,' he murmured, his eyes watchful.

'You frighten me!' She stopped short, shaking and furious, then snatched up the piece of paper and flung it on to the floor. The lute-player did not pause in her peaceful gentle melody. 'Do you think you've given me pleasure by revealing this to me?' she demanded fiercely.

'How you use the information is immaterial to me,' he said, the cold hint of steel in his smile. 'It is certainly not my intention to give you pleasure, no. My intention is simply to show you how completely alone you are.'

He paused to let that sink in. It chilled her to the bone.

'I've got William,' she said shakily.

'Cattermole is an old man,' he rejoined smoothly. 'Nevertheless, if I were you, I should inform him—and the police—of Gomez's dealings as soon as possible. There is a chance ...' he drank from his wine with relish '... a very small chance—that you will be able to recover a few thousands of your stolen money from Mr Gomez.' She stared at him, speechless. 'Of course,' he added, 'that would do little more than prolong Westlake's final agony for a week or so. The end is very close, Sabrina.'

'But why do you *want* Westlake?' she asked desperately. 'What will you do with it once you have it?'

'Plough it into the ground,' he said calmly. She blinked in disbelief.

'*What?*'

'I intend to destroy it utterly.' He watched her reaction without expression. 'The whole thing. Discharge the workers first of all. After that, I shall dismantle every factory, sell off the machines, and use dynamite to destroy the buildings. Then plough the rubble into the ground with bulldozers. Create a wasteland out of each of the twenty-three plants and factories across this country—so that in ten years' time no one will even remember the name of Westlake.' He smiled calmly. 'That's what I want Westlake for.'

'I don't believe you,' she whispered, stunned.

'It makes excellent economic sense,' he said, lacing his fingers together as coolly as though he were discussing a chess-game. 'It'll only take me a year to fill the gap with my own products. My biggest rival will have disappeared as though it had never existed, and I'll have won over the lion's share of a very lucrative and expanding market. And my increased profits will be measured in tens of millions, Sabrina. A colossal fortune.'

She stared blindly at him for long seconds, then stood up, white and trembling. 'I want my coat,' she said unsteadily. 'I've got to speak to William!'

'Sit down,' he said, and the steel in his voice cut through her near-hysteria. 'There is nothing you can do at this time of night. And we have much to discuss.' Slowly, she lowered herself on to the seat again. The deep red of her gown contrasted vividly with the pallor of her skin now, and even the diamond at her throat seemed to have lost its brilliant sparkle. But there was no pity in Leonardo l'Aquila's face. He poured her a small glass of dark liqueur from the bottle on the table. 'Drink,' he commanded, and she obeyed numbly. The thick sweet alcohol scalded her throat, bringing a little colour back to her face. She closed her long-lashed lids over her eyes and leaned back, giddy with shock.

'How beautiful you are,' he said gently; yet she knew that had she been watching, she would have seen that the grey eyes held no softness in their bright depths as they lingered on the vulnerable curve of her lovely throat. 'You look like some pre-Raphaelite painting, my dear Sabrina—*Dido on the Funeral Pyre*, perhaps—or *Leda and the Swan.*'

With an effort, she opened her deep blue eyes and stared at him.

'You can't do this, Signor l'Aquila——'

'Leo,' he corrected gently. She grimaced in distaste.

'Leo,' she repeated, the word like poison on her numbed lips. 'It's inhuman. You'll be putting thousands of people out of work, causing untold misery. You simply *can't.*'

'I anticipate a little trouble with the Monopolies Commission—but nothing my legal department can't handle.' He poured more liqueur into her glass. 'Believe me, Ice Maiden, I can do it, and I will do it.'

'What is it you want?' she asked urgently. 'To leave Westlake alone. To reprieve all those people whose lives and futures you now control. What will it take to stop you?'

'Your turn of phrase is quite touching,' he said, a drop of acid in his deep purr. 'Since when did any Westlake care a tinker's curse about those who worked for him?'

'Just because I bear Simon Westlake's name doesn't mean that I'm anything like him! What you're suggesting is monstrous! It's unspeakable!'

'It's just business.' He leaned forward and lifted the big diamond from its chain around her neck, and held it up before her face so that its dazzling light danced in the ultramarine depths of her eyes.

'A pretty bauble,' he said gently. 'Your badge of office.' His eyes took in her beautiful clothes speculatively. 'You obviously enjoy your wealth.'

'I make my own clothes, as you know. I've never used my wealth.' Hating the way he'd managed to put her on the defensive, she shrugged angrily. How could she ever tell anyone, least of all this man, what it had been like to be Simon Westlake's daughter? 'I am my father's daughter,' she said heavily. 'And I'm damned if I'm going to justify myself to you.'

'Yes,' he said softly, 'you are your father's daughter, Sabrina Westlake. You have his pride, his strength of will.' When he smiled now, his even, white teeth were almost savage, as though he could have buried them in her soft throat and torn out her life with pleasure.

'If it's money you want,' she said dully, 'I can give you whatever personal fortune my father left me.'

'Indeed?' he asked calmly, the mocking light back in his beautiful eyes. 'What have you got?' She glanced involuntarily at his commanding, passionate mouth. Could a man with such a mouth really be so cruel, so callous? Yet her father himself had been a handsome man. The Devil himself was reputed to be handsome.

'You know what I have,' she said in a low, bitter voice. 'The house at Winfields, fourteen or fifteen acres of land. Some antiques. Three horses. I don't know what else. No doubt you've already assessed their value to the last penny.'

'Not quite. But it's an impressive little catalogue for a woman of twenty-two.' He took the coffee-tray from Mei-Ling, and poured two measures into the gilt and enamel cups. 'I'm afraid that all these possessions of yours cannot be worth more than a million pounds, my dear Sabrina. Westlake is in hock for much, much more. If Cressida launches its new programme on schedule next week, you'll need more like five million pounds. And that means obliteration—either at the hands of the official Receiver, or under the blades of my bulldozers.'

She watched him with fascinated eyes, her thick lashes wet with unshed tears. 'So,' he smiled, watching her in return over the rim of his coffee-cup, 'what else can you offer?'

'You take a great deal of pleasure in this game, don't you?' she said, her voice quivering with emotion.

'Pleasure? That word is not accurate, I'm afraid. Satisfaction, perhaps.'

'Your satisfaction is cruel, remorseless,' she said. She looked blindly around the Oriental splendour of the room, the calm figure of the lute-player, her head still bent peacefully to her melodies. 'Can you really enjoy the thought of causing such destruction, such misery?'

'If you are to ask such intimate questions,' he said with another calm sip of his coffee, 'then you really must start calling me Leo. But you still haven't answered my question, Sabrina fair. What else do you possess?'

'Nothing,' she whispered and the word hung on the air like a sigh. Leonardo l'Aquila put down his cup and considered her thoughtfully.

'Nothing. Quite so. Yet if I choose to hold back my wolves, none of the destruction and misery you talk about need occur. If I cancel Cressida's new programme, stop competing with Westlake for the electronics market—then your corporation will continue as before. There will be chaos,' he smiled grimly, 'when the honest Roderigo is sacked and the prosecution against him gets under way. But Westlake will survive. More than that—if Westlake joins with Cressida to form a single corporate force, uniting our technology and manpower, then Westlake will survive with its strength redoubled. Your precious employees will not only be safe, but will find themselves with higher pay than they have ever known. And your personal position on the very pinnacle of the pyramid, my dear Sabrina, will be safe.' He reached out, picking up her limp hand, and studied the open palm with hooded eyes. She waited, hope and fear struggling in her heart. 'For this,' he went on, 'I ask a price.'

'What price?'

'I want you, Sabrina Westlake. Only you. Nothing else.'

She looked at him blankly, trying to fathom his meaning. 'Me? But how can you possibly *have* me?'

'As my wife,' he said calmly.

The cold shock of his words drained through her system, and she jerked her hand out of his fingers. 'Your sense of the humorous is decidedly perverse, Signor,' she snapped. 'Are you trying to make a fool of me yet again?'

'Not at all.' He leaned on one elbow, smiling slightly. 'I'm very serious indeed. Would you prefer me to go down on one knee?'

'I don't believe it.' A numb, dreamlike feeling made her shiver helplessly. Marriage? What on earth did he mean? There must be some new, even more subtle torment behind his strange words. 'What—what possible reason do you have for asking such an extraordinary thing of me?'

'Perhaps I've fallen madly in love with you,' he suggested, eyes still smiling into hers.

'And perhaps the moon is made of green cheese!' She was growing angry now. She'd been expecting some business proposal, an offer of a merger or an affiliation, not this blatantly calculated personal insult. 'May I ask where your home is, Signor l'Aquila?'

'In Capri,' he replied. The most beautiful island in the Mediterranean. Why do you ask?'

'Capri,' she repeated, having a vision of some primitive, goat-ridden island community. 'I have no idea what barbarous customs are in force for choosing a wife in Capri—but in England, Signor, blackmail is illegal!' His lazy smile infuriated her. 'No doubt it amuses you to upset me like this. You aren't serious in the slightest, whatever you say!'

'Oh, but I am.' His voice was velvety. 'If you think I haven't been serious in one thing I've said tonight, Sabrina, you're making a very dangerous mistake indeed.'

'You want to marry me?' She shook her head in bewilderment. 'For God's sake, what for?'

'I want you. On my terms.'

'As a chattel?' she challenged. Her eyes were fierce, reflecting the wildly defensive posture her heart was taking. 'Like some winner's trophy, to prove you've beaten Westlake?'

He laughed with genuine amusement. 'How dramatic you are sometimes. I could beat a dozen Westlakes, Sabrina. I only want you.'

'But you're talking about a *marriage*, not some kind of technical arrangement!' She twisted her slender fingers nervously. 'A marriage means living together, man and wife. How long do you think a marriage like the one you're proposing would last? And what will happen when you grow tired of your little game? A quick divorce? You must see that it's impossible, it can't be done!'

'That's your final word?' he asked indifferently.

'It must be,' she said, her voice almost pleading. 'Think of some other price, anything——'

'There is no other price.' He drained his glass. 'You might as well say goodbye to Westlake now, then. Because Westlake is doomed, Sabrina. I'll not leave one stone of it standing upon another.'

'*No!*' The cry was wrung from her. 'You can't do it!'

'Well well.' One eyebrow arched mockingly. 'Signs of real emotion at last. You must be very fond of wealth and power.'

'Destroying Westlake means putting tens of thousands out of work,' she gasped, seeing the devastation in her mind's eye. It was too horrible to contemplate. 'For the love of God, how can you balance all those people's careers against me?' She shook her head dizzily. 'I'm not worth all that destruction, all that misery! It's insane.'

'Your choice is clear, then.' Broodingly, his eyes watched her from an impassive bronze mask. 'Am I so repulsive to you?'

'That isn't the point,' she burst out.

'Am I?' he demanded.

'Of course not.' She made a futile gesture. 'You're physically beautiful, and you know it. But...'

Again he laughed with unaffected pleasure, amusement warming those cold grey eyes. 'You've had even less experience of men than I imagined, Sabrina. You find me attractive?'

She flushed deeply, hating his supreme confidence. 'I didn't say that. I said that you weren't repulsive.'

'And there are no men in your life, are there? Unless we count the young squires of Berkshire who've been sniffing round you these past few months.' He shrugged. 'What obstacle can there be to our marriage?'

'You're unbelievable. People don't get married just because there's no obstacle! And there *is* an

obstacle here—the fact that you're holding a gun
to my head!'

'Well.' He made a chopping motion with one
hand, as though terminating the argument. 'Let it
not be said that I forced you into marriage—even
though I do come from Capri.' His eyes glinted.
'I give you three days to make your mind up,
Sabrina. By Sunday night I want your answer.
And on Sunday there must be no more evasion,
you understand?'

She had to nod, that dreamlike feeling coming
over her again.

'Listen to me,' he said softly, his face intent.
'The next three days may well be the most
important in your life. No other decision you take
will have such far-reaching consequences as this
one. You spoke of divorce a few minutes ago.
That word does not exist in my vocabulary,
Sabrina. So think—and think well.'

As she walked in a daze through the darkened
hallway at Winfields, the telephone was ringing
shrilly in its alcove.

It was William Cattermole, sounding dis-
traught, spilling out the news that Roderigo
Gomez had disappeared—it was thought to
Mexico—leaving a horrible financial tangle
behind him. 'The unbelievable part,' William
said, sounding old, 'is that he seems to have been
stealing from the Corporation for months. What
happened tonight, Sabrina? Did l'Aquila make an
offer for Westlake?'

'Something like that,' she said dully. 'How did
the news about Roderigo break?'

'Through the computers. This afternoon, the whole story came up on our screens, all neatly laid out and documented. It was too late. Roderigo's gone, Sabrina—and there's no automatic extradition from Mexico——'

'I know.' She closed her eyes in weary disgust. It was true, then. Somewhere deep inside she'd been hoping that l'Aquila had been lying about Roderigo. 'Is there the faintest chance of getting any of our money back?'

'No.' The monosyllable was despairing. 'I blame myself. I've failed you, Sabrina, failed the Corporation, failed you both so badly...'

'You couldn't help it,' she said with a flicker of a smile. 'Roderigo was far more cunning than either of us. It took a sharper mind to ferret him out.'

'What do you mean?'

'Our friend the Eagle knew all about Roderigo. He's known for months—he must have penetrated our codes ages ago. He actually presented me with the evidence over dinner tonight.' She closed her eyes, a wave of giddiness passing over her again. 'l'Aquila's been watching Roderigo for months, laughing up his sleeve while Roderigo ate Westlake away from the inside, making his take-over all the easier.'

'My God.'

'Oh, Leo l'Aquila's very cool,' she said in a strained voice. 'You have to admire him for it.'

'You realise this makes us totally helpless?' William asked. 'We're in l'Aquila's pocket now, Sabrina. He's outmanouevred us on every front. The only hope we've got left now is an appeal to the Monopolies Commission, but that won't stop Westlake from collapsing——'

'We don't have any hope left, William. It's funny. A short time ago Westlake was all-powerful, impregnable. Now we're on the edge of ruin. Like so many other empires, not so, William? There really wasn't a fight at all, was there?' She'd once thought she hated her father, but now she'd found out what hate *really* was. Hate was falling under the shadow of a man like Leo l'Aquila.

'Are you all right?' he asked urgently. 'You sound terrible, Sabrina!'

'I feel terrible.' It was all like a nightmare now, an endless dream from which there was no awakening. 'But the crisis is over. There'll be no more conflict with Cressida.'

'What on earth do you mean?'

'I'm getting married. Soon, I don't know when. That's his price.' She laughed, a brittle sound. 'William, I'll speak to you tomorrow. Right now I'm going for a ride.'

She replaced the receiver before the stunned William had time to gabble out another question, and walked as if in a trance to the stables.

Under a white moon, she urged Criterion into a fast trot across the virgin snow. Married! To a man as ruthless and selfish as her father had been!

Who in God's name could she turn to? She'd thought of Clarry, and had longed for her friend's companionship and comfort; but she'd also known that Clarry would never be able to understand the exact position she was in.

Anyway, how could Clarry help? How could anyone help? This was her fight, her tragedy, and she was going to have to face it—and resolve it—in her own way. Not Clarry, not William, not anyone she knew could help her now.

And her life stretched ahead of her, lonelier and more isolated than ever before.

But when had it been any different? She kicked at Criterion's flanks with her bare heels, and he broke into a canter, his shivering muscles betraying his sympathetic nervousness.

Did she really have any choice? Her mind was almost too tired to reason. If she didn't marry him, she was calling down obliteration for Westlake and every soul in the Corporation's employ. Personal obliteration, too. Living with herself wouldn't be easy after the catastrophe Leo had planned for all of them. Living as Leo's wife might be even more terrible.

Why? Why did he want her? She gripped Criterion's mane in her fingers, and rode him swiftly through the ghostly fields, his hooves thudding hollow on the silent ground. Was it possible that he could really desire her? After all, she had what would conventionally be called beauty. And yet, to go to such great lengths, merely for the sake of capturing her—she couldn't believe anyone could possibly desire her to that extent. What was she, after all? One inexperienced woman, almost a girl, with none of the wiles or allure that might have enslaved a man as sophisticated as l'Aquila.

Yet supposing he *did* desire her. Maybe even, in his terrible way, love her. The thought sent a strange feeling through her veins, part fear, part something else. Was it triumph? Even a responding sexual and emotional chord? He was physically beautiful, as desirable a man as any dream could produce. But ruthless, possessing a power to hurt and destroy like nothing else she'd known. Could she ever be happy with a man like that?

How like Simon Westlake he had been tonight, how merciless and hard and triumphant!

She kicked Criterion into a gallop, his broad back thudding hard against her thighs as she clung to his surging neck. Suddenly she didn't want to think any more, didn't want to remember the way he had dominated her tonight, bent her will.

They raced through the icy air, the wind lifting the velvet of her dress and floating it out behind her, exposing her long legs, her midnight-black hair streaming back, darker than the night. They reached the edge of the wood, flying like the wind, and among the trees the big horse stumbled, pitching her off into the deep snow. She staggered to her feet, unhurt, and ran over to Criterion. He, too, was uninjured, but he was trembling violently, and his breath was blowing plumes of steam into the still air.

The snow was deadly cold on her bare legs, but she did not care. She clung to the horse's big, comforting neck, pressing her face to his shuddering skin, and clung there. Leo had been right—there was no man in her life. There never would be, in all probability; having a father like Simon Westlake hadn't disposed her to regard the institution of marriage with any reverence.

She had no illusions, at least. She was very likely an emotional cripple, anyway. Emotionally frigid. Incapable of giving or receiving warmth. In twenty-two years she'd never been attracted to any man. Maybe this was the best way—a cold, arranged marriage with a total stranger. A marriage devoid of those treacherous delusions, trust and love. Maybe that would be the only kind of marriage she'd ever be able to cope with.

She climbed back on to the horse, and turned his head homewards. She was bitterly chilled, and yet she now knew that there was no choice. He hadn't left her any. Utterly alone in this world, she'd never had much choice, had she?

The tears that stained her cheeks were clawed away in the wind, scattered on the unseeing night.

CHAPTER FOUR

'I DON'T believe it,' Sabrina said furiously. She turned to him, dark smudges of weariness under her eyes. 'You expect me to play hostess to a dinner-party for your damned friends—on the day we arrive from England?'

'My friends are not damned,' he replied mildly, unloosening his tie. 'At least not too many of them, I hope. And they will be most eager to meet you.'

'I refuse point-blank,' she said, almost stamping her foot in frustration. She slumped tiredly into a white leather armchair. The flight from Heathrow had been short, but her exhaustion was primarily emotional. The events of the past few days had become a whirl which even now confused her. Since her arrival in Capri an hour ago, she had barely had time to sort her thoughts out; and a minute ago he had calmly informed her that they were entertaining eight of his friends to a formal dinner that night. 'It's out of the question,' she went on, her voice slightly hysterical. 'You can't expect me to arrive here at midday and be playing lady of the manor by evening!'

'It's out of the question for you to refuse,' he said dangerously. 'The invitations were issued days ago. Sabrina, we've known each other for some time now.'

'If you can call a ruthless pursuit knowing,' she retorted.

'The pursuit is over,' he pointed out. 'England is far behind you now. With the injection of capital from Cressida, Westlake will go from strength to strength. Gomez is being prosecuted— my lawyer Bianchi is seeing to that. So you have no more worries. It's time to leave that world behind you, and realise that you are living in a new one now.' His voice became gentler. 'If you need rest, have an hour or two's sleep now. Come.' He stretched out his hand imperiously. 'I'll show you to the bedroom.'

'Can't I have another cup of coffee, for God's sake?' She rested her forehead in her hand. A headache was throbbing behind her eyes, intensifying her sense of confusion and loss. Talk of bedrooms only made her feel worse. 'I can hardly think straight.'

'You think too much anyway,' he said with a smile. 'I'll order some coffee.'

'I can still hardly believe any of this.' She lay back, dull eyes wandering around the room. Of the last few days, only isolated incidents bobbed up in her mind. The stark simplicity of the registry-office ceremony, and the spark of grey fire in Leonardo's eyes as he had slipped the wedding-ring over her trembling finger. The warmth of his lips against the coldness of her own. William Cattermole's troubled eyes, the unspoken questions she could see hovering on his tongue. They'd left for Capri within hours.

She'd hardly had time to notice her surroundings, except that the villa was set among tall pines overlooking the sea. It was made of white marble, and from the car that had brought them from the airport, it had looked as cool as a house of ice. A very efficient house; servants had been ready to collect their suitcases as they arrived, and coffee with almond cakes had been prepared at once.

She stood up and walked across to the wide French window leading on to the vine-covered patio, and stared across the silvery surface of the Mediterranean.

Leonardo l'Aquila's home was exquisite, with its striking interior designs and its beautiful, terraced garden leading down to the cliffs and the calm sea below. In another time and place, she might have loved it. She rested her forehead on the cold glass, tired out. The servants had already disappeared with her three suitcases. That was all he had allowed her to take from Winfields. And the great echoing mansion had been shut up, the shutters closed on its gloomy memories and secrets for ever.

Sabrina l'Aquila. They had made so striking a couple coming out of the registry office that almost none of the dailies had been able to resist publishing the picture. He, tall and magnificent, a smile curving those passionate lips, the grey eyes level and commanding; she, tremblingly beautiful in her plain white suit, her raven's-wing hair framing her oval face, long lashes shading downcast eyes. The perfect couple! No wonder all the gossip magazines had gone into yapping hysteria as dozens of photographers upturned boxes of old photographs, dozens of reporters flicked through past newspapers, trying to trace

the origins of this, the most glamorous, most
romantic, most astonishing match of the year.
And how many envious eyes had fallen on the
famous pictures of the bride and groom emerging
from the registry office!

But no one knew. No one knew the agony in
her heart, the tears that pricked so close behind
her lids. Or the steel bite of his fingers in her
arm, his purr in her ear, 'Smile, *sposa mia*. Give
the jackals their money's worth.'

She heard him come back into the room, heard
the clink of coffee-cups. 'Don't make me do it,'
she pleaded quietly. 'I'll meet your friends some
other time, Signor.'

'Let's not have a scene.' His voice was
good-humoured, but the threat was there none
the less. She flinched as his hand closed around
her arm. 'I want to show you the house,
Sabrina. Come.'

'If you insist,' she said petulantly. But as she
allowed him to escort her through the airy halls,
she told herself that starting from now, she would
never again surrender to his will. Not in the way
he wanted her to.

The room he led her to was massive and
beautiful, furnished in a deep butter yellow, with
heavy silk drapes and coverings of the same
colour. The bed in the centre of the room was
enormous, a stately four-poster tented with
luxurious yellow silk.

'Is this my bedroom?' she asked, taken aback.

'Yours?' he smiled drily. 'It's for both of us,
girl.'

'You're joking!' This was something she had

not considered. 'You don't mean to share the same bedroom as me?'

'It's not unknown between married couples,' he said gently.

She had never shared any kind of intimacy with anyone before, let alone someone so aggressively male as Leo, and the thought appalled her. 'This won't do!' she said furiously. 'I demand to have a separate bedroom.'

He lay back on the sunshine-yellow quilt to smile gently at her.

'You insist, you demand, you refuse. Not very domestic words, Sabrina. You aren't addressing a Westlake board-meeting now.'

'I never thought I was,' she spat. The idea of undressing before him, of getting into the same bed, made her flesh crawl. 'If you had any respect——'

'You are in no position to demand anything, Sabrina,' he said softly. The glint in his grey eyes hinted that his patience was slipping. 'Try and remember that you are my wife, now. Why not get some rest before the party?' He got to his feet lithely, and began undressing.

'What are you doing?' she demanded in alarm.

'I'm taking a shower. Care to join me?'

'I'd sooner shower with a tiger-shark,' she retorted. 'I'm not getting into that bed with you, not tonight nor anytime. You must have them make up a bed for me elsewhere, Leo!'

He turned to her, his mouth brutally set.

'*Must?* That is not a word to use to a husband, my beloved wife.' He stalked to the mahogany cupboards and threw the doors open, revealing all her clothes neatly hanging, her underwear folded in the drawers. 'Look, Sabrina—there are your clothes. This is your bedroom—and here you will sleep.'

'I will not!' she hissed, all her pent-up hatred of the man boiling in her veins.

'Then, by God, you will not sleep at all.' The fierce retort took her breath away. She stared from him to the neat rows of her own garments, so carefully packed in the cupboard. Dear God, what was going to become of her?

He continued undressing, as indifferent to her as though she'd been a cat. She knew almost nothing about men, had never wanted to know. But she knew that Leo was magnificently male. She watched in fascination as he stripped, clinging to the bedpost with hands whose damp palms contradicted her dry throat. He was lithe, tanned, dark-nippled and dark-haired; so little spare flesh on his big frame that every muscle, from the thickest to the most delicate, was outlined under the mahogany velvet of his skin.

Giddily, she found herself wondering whether he would be hard, like the oak or bronze he seemed to be carved from. The thought made her shiver, and he looked across at her with mocking eyes.

'You look like a ghost, my dear. Can it be you've never seen a man undress before?'

She turned away, her face suffused with scarlet, and his silky laughter trailed across her skin. 'I'm going to shower. Get some rest, Sabrina. You're overwrought.'

She heard the bathroom door shut, and

afterwards the muted rustle of the shower. Tired and despairing, she kicked her shoes off, and curled up on the bed. A wave of home-sickness unfolded inside her, almost bringing back the tears she'd sworn never to let out again. The thought of facing a company of strangers tonight was unbearable. What a farce it would be! How the hell was she expected to meet their enquiring eyes? How could she pretend that her marriage to Leo was anything but what it was—a tragic charade? Sleep came mercifully, helping to ease the pain of a separation from home, familiar places, and such friends as she'd ever had.

The party was, extraordinarily enough, a complete success. She'd expected Leo's friends to be elderly businessmen, coldly curious about, and probably hostile towards, his English bride. Instead, they were mostly young, lively people. Vittoria Valenti, an actress Sabrina had seen in several films, was undoubtedly the most glamorous, while her charming producer-husband Carlo was, in his forties, the oldest of the party. But the other two couples, Lucio and Sara Schiaparelli, and the Ferraris, who seemed always to be laughing, could scarcely have been kinder or warmer towards Sabrina.

She hadn't expected to be amused tonight, but by mid-evening she realised that she'd seldom been so entertained in her life. The dinner had emerged from the kitchen in perfect order, Leo had been a splendidly genial host, and the conversation—held mostly in English for her sake—had been fascinating and hilarious by turns.

The only unattached person in the party was a distant cousin of Leo's, a slim, rather plain brunette called Michaela Torino, who had been seated at Sabrina's end of the table. Unlike the others—Lucio Schiaparelli and his wife were both architects and Bruno Ferrari a writer—Michaela was still a student. That gave Sabrina something in common with her, and as the conversation broadened out over the dessert, Sabrina turned to her with a smile.

'What's Rome University like? Wonderfully stimulating, I expect?'

'Very crowded,' Michaela laughed, 'but stimulating, as you say. You were at Manchester weren't you?'

'For three years,' Sabrina nodded. 'I did English Literature, but it never came to much use. Half-way through my degree I realised that I wasn't cut out to be a teacher. Dress-designing appealed much more! So as soon as I graduated, I started a design shop with some friends.'

'Is that your own design?' Michaela looked admiringly at the grey silk evening-dress as Sabrina nodded. 'It's beautiful. I love the, how do you call it, the collar?'

'Thank you.'

'But your dress business—it didn't last long, yes? You inherited your father's factories.'

'That's right.'

Michaela's soft brown eyes were questioning. 'Is that how you met Leo?'

'Yes,' Sabrina said with an inner touch of

wryness. 'That's how I met Leo.'

'I think it's so *romantic*,' Michaela sighed. Her expression was envious. 'You're so lucky, Sabrina—to have wealth *and* a man like Leonardo l'Aquila for your husband.'

'Extraordinary luck,' Sabrina agreed, though she didn't say what kind. She felt Leo's eyes on her, and answered his smile from the other end of the table. Was he laughing at her? Sara Schiaparelli broke away from her conversation with the actress and leaned towards Sabrina.

'Quite a whirlwind romance, indeed! It couldn't be more romantic, Sabrina.'

'No,' Sabrina said, still smiling. If only they knew quite how strange her marriage really was.

'How long have you known Leo?' Michaela asked.

'A matter of weeks. It was such a whirlwind romance,' she added ironically, 'that I scarcely know anything about my husband!'

'Don't worry, you're not the only one.' Carlo Valenti had caught her words, and grinned at her, his handsome face a mass of wrinkles. 'Leo's a man of mystery.'

'Exactly,' his wife pouted. 'We've known you for years, Leo, and yet you hardly ever talk about your childhood, where you were born, your parents, anything like that.'

'I'm a self-made man,' Leo said. His eyes touched Sabrina's for a second, then glanced smilingly away. '*Ipso facto*, I dispensed with parents.'

'Not good enough,' Sara Schiaparelli complained. 'There's some mystery here. Let me guess.' She leaned forward, cupping her chin in her palm, and studied Leo with liquid eyes. He returned her gaze solemnly, his faint smile still in place. 'With that face and physique,' she decided, 'your origins can't be entirely mortal.'

'Not entirely moral?' Leo grinned.

'Not entirely *mortal*. And that's the secret you've been hiding all these years! Your father must have been a god—one of those gods who come down and ravish peasant girls in all the old legends.'

'The question is,' Carlo Valenti mused, 'which of the gods? Mars?'

'With those grey eyes, more likely Neptune,' Lucia Ferrari put in. She gave Sabrina an artful glance. 'Sabrina will know best of all. We appeal to you—which of the gods was Leo's father?'

'That's easy.' Sabrina looked at her husband's handsome face and smiled tightly. 'Vulcan.'

'Vulcan?' Sara pulled a face. 'He was lame.'

'But he was the artificer of the gods,' Carlo said, nodding. 'The great technician. Blacksmith, armourer, designer. Yes, I think Sabrina's hit the nail on the head.'

Leo's eyes were still on hers, the contact making her shiver inside. How compelling his gaze was!

'Are we right?' Sabrina demanded.

'I'm flattered.' At last he drew his eyes away from Sabrina's and smiled around the table. 'No, my parents were human, like all of yours. It's just that they died young, and in sad circumstances. I seldom talk about them.'

There was a silence, and then Sabrina leaned

forward. 'Oh, Leo, I'm so sorry.' Her eyes were big and dark. 'I didn't mean to bring up a sad memory.'

'Please. It's nothing.' He tilted his head on one side, still watching her, and in that moment she felt closer to him than she'd ever done before. They had that in common, at least—a childhood clouded by sorrow.

As if to make up for the uncomfortable moment, everyone started talking simultaneously, and the exchange was soon forgotten.

Not by Sabrina. Something in his face haunted her for a long while. Some shadow in his smile. She'd felt instinctively that, like her, Leo was acquainted with grief. It was something she had to get to the bottom of, as soon as she could.

In deference to their having only arrived from England that day, the party broke up around eleven. The effervescent Ferraris were the last to leave, and as their tail-lights disappeared through the cypresses, Sabrina felt Leo's arm encircle her waist. Stiffening, she tried to pull away.

'Why so tense?' he enquired, leading her back into the house. 'Wedding-night nerves?'

She didn't find the joke in very good taste, and kept an obstinate silence while he locked up.

The bedroom was warm and welcoming, but her heart was beating unpleasantly as he switched off the glittering crystals of the main light, leaving the room bathed in a warm, peachy glow from the two bedside lamps.

'You seemed to enjoy the evening after all,' he said, making it a question. He was casually undressing, and she looked away.

'It was all right,' she admitted stiffly. 'I'm sorry if I upset you with all that rubbish about your parents.'

'Sara's sense of humour is always a little odd,' he shrugged. 'She once had rather a heavy crush on me.'

'Is that so?' The news didn't improve her mood, and she found an excuse to toy moodily with the bottles she'd laid out on the white dressing-table.

'Do you intend to sleep with your boots on, like a Cossack?' he enquired mildly. She caught a glimpse of him in the mirror, the dark hair on his naked body disturbingly pagan as he slid between the sheets. Damn him! Was he wearing anything? He probably expected her to sleep naked with him. Probably expected her to submit to his love-making . . .

The thought ignited unreasoning anger in her. Her delicate skin still flushed, she went to the cupboard, and wrenched out the first nightdress she could lay her hands on, then stalked into the adjoining bathroom and slammed the door behind her. In the marble splendour she tore her clothes off, muttering curses under her breath, and prepared for bed. She'd been dreading this situation all evening. What a wedding-night! She examined her flushed face in the mirror. Her black hair was tumbled untidily about her eyes, which were still gleaming with anger. She wasn't going to let him make love to her tonight. Nor ever.

Her body was her own, wasn't it? She took a deep breath, switched off the bathroom light, and walked back into the bedroom, combing her long black hair with angry, vigorous strokes.

'Are you always going to order me around,' she demanded, not looking at him, 'like your captive?'

'Not a captive,' he told her, his eyes studying the outline of her slender figure through the thin material of her nightdress. 'A wife.'

'A wife?' she scorned. 'Even though this marriage is only a mockery?'

'Is it indeed?' he asked softly as she came to sit on the far edge of the wide bed, staring at him with resentful blue eyes. 'We shall see how much of a mockery it is, my sweet.'

The hands that reached for her were irresistibly strong, and she yelped in alarm as he hauled her across the silk sheets to him.

'Let me go——'

He was ruthlessly strong, thrusting her back against the pillows, pinning her there with the hard pressure of his chest. His grey eyes stared down at hers with fire in their splendid depths.

'This marriage is no mockery,' he said quietly, with a hint of steel in his voice.

'You're hurting me,' she gasped. 'You don't know how strong you are—you frighten me sometimes, Leo!'

'My poor innocent,' he mocked, and then bent to kiss her, his mouth firm and hard. 'You kiss like a virgin,' he purred, his lips finding hers again. Frantic, she dug her nails into his back as hard as she could, not caring whether she drew blood. In response his hand twisted ruthlessly in the thickness of her hair, making her cry out with pain. He raised himself on one elbow to look down at her flushed face.

'Are you?' he demanded. 'Have you ever slept with a man?'

'You know I never have,' she said bitterly. She turned her head aside to hide the wetness on her long lashes. 'Only a base coward would hurt a woman.'

He rolled her gently but firmly on to her back, and looked at her seriously. 'Sabrina,' he said in his deep voice, 'let us get one thing perfectly straight—tonight and for ever. If you hurt me, I shall hurt you in return. I have no qualms, no compunction about inflicting pain on a woman, especially not a daughter of Simon Westlake. So keep your claws sheathed—and I shall sheathe mine. Do you understand?'

'You make the rules,' she whispered bitterly, looking up into the magnificent face above her.

'Excellent.' He caressed the cloudy hair out of her eyes with a hand so gentle that she shuddered briefly despite herself. 'And tonight, I assure you, it is not my intention to inflict pain upon you.'

His lips were warm and gentle now, taking hers with an authority that she could not refuse. She tried briefly to struggle, but he was firm, commanding. His tongue pressed against her teeth, thrusting past them into the sweetness of her inner mouth—and something stirred deep inside her, for the first time. He felt it, and was smiling as he leaned back.

'You once said I attracted you. Do I still attract you?'

'Don't do this to me,' she said in a low voice. 'There can be no pleasure where there's force.'

'I don't intend to use force,' he assured her in amusement. 'Only kindness.'

'Save your sweet talk for your mistresses,' she retorted.

His eyes narrowed smokily. 'Mistresses?' he rasped.

'I presume you have dozens,' she retorted bravely. 'Like Sara Schiaparelli maybe? Well, satisfy your lust on them, Leo. Because you may as well know here and now that I'll never let you use me as your whore.'

The minute the words left her lips, she regretted them bitterly. Spoken half in fear, they had been meant to turn aside the desire she could see so plainly in Leo's face. But the way his fingers bit into her shoulders alarmed her.

'You little vixen,' he said softly. 'Who taught you to have such words on your soft lips?'

'That is how you intend to use me, isn't it?' she quavered. 'You brought me back from England like the spoils of a battle. A bought whore to prove your manhood on.'

'You defile the marriage-bed with such talk,' he said icily. 'Let us have no more of it.'

Suddenly, it had all become too much for her. Exhaustion, loneliness, tension had all taken their toll of her nerves. She tried to choke back the sob, but it rose up saltily nonetheless, and the tears welled up uncontrollably, and spilled across her pale cheeks.

He raised an eyebrow in surprise at her tears.

'What a strange creature you are,' he

murmured. 'You're all contrasts—now crying, now snarling, now the tigress, now the lamb. I do not understand you.'

He drew her close, and it was heaven to have a broad, male-scented shoulder to cry on. She clung to him, forgetting for a few minutes who he was and what he had done to her, and allowed herself the luxury of crying on the chest of a strong man.

Leo cradled her with astonishing tenderness, one hand caressing her hair, her jerking shoulders, until she lay still against him, her mind numb. His compassion overwhelmed her. It was almost impossible to believe that this was the same man whose mockery could cut through her thin skin like a lash. She clung to him, burying her grief in his comfort, taking solace from his caress.

'I'm so—tired,' she said shakily. 'I'm sorry if—I was—hysterical. It's all been—a bit much.'

'Of course it has,' he murmured. 'It's I who should be sorry, my love. Rest now, close your eyes.' She obeyed, feeling like a child. 'You were charming tonight,' he went on softly. 'So beautiful, so graceful. You made me proud of you.'

She snuggled into his chest, feeling sleep welling up in her mind. Distantly, she was aware of her arms and legs giving little twitches as tense muscles unwound.

'I'm so—tired,' she whispered, her mouth going slack.

'Then sleep, my love.'

Peace drifted over her.

$\star$ $\star$ $\star$

The Mediterranean breeze blew cool off the grey sea, along the beach, up the cliffs, and through the tall cypresses in the garden. In the rough leather coat he'd put on, Leo looked more like a spectacularly handsome shepherd than the high-powered businessman who'd just taken over a massive Corporation.

Sabrina clung to his hand as they clambered over the boulders near the edge of the cliff, surrounded by wheeling gulls.

'Is this safe?' she asked anxiously.

'Safer than being in bed, apparently,' he said, flashing her a grin. 'The wind's put some colour in your cheeks. You look almost healthy.'

'Don't I always?' She scrambled up on to the promontory he had chosen, and clung to his arm as she took in the sheer view down to the sea. 'How lovely!' The island was set like a jewel just out of the Bay of Naples, and the dim outline of the mainland rose up to the white-capped peak of Vesuvius in the high distance. 'No wonder rich and famous people congregate here!'

'This is my eyrie,' he smiled. 'My refuge.'

'You don't need to take refuge from anything,' she retorted. Underneath the well-worn leather, the muscles of his arm were taut with raw power. Yet, glancing at him now, Sabrina thought that he had changed since they had left London. Here, in his own home in Italy, the lines of tension around his eyes had faded, and the fierce set of that level mouth had eased slightly.

Neither of them had mentioned last night so far. He'd let her sleep late, and a business colleague and his young wife had arrived for lunch, forestalling any intimate conversation. Leo obviously led a busy social life. She'd liked these people, the Rossinis, even more than the people who'd come last night, but the sense of inner disturbance resulting from last night's conflict had prevented her from relaxing fully. This afternoon's walk through the massive garden to the cliff's edge had been exactly what she needed to clear her mind.

'You're so lucky.' She turned to look over his shoulder at the villa above them. 'This place is magnificent, Leo.'

'I'll have to build a fence here one day,' he said, gazing along the line of the cliff.

'Why? That would spoil it.'

'It wouldn't be safe for children,' he explained.

'I suppose not.' The sudden thought that he might be talking about *her* children sent a strange, disturbing feeling through her stomach. 'I suppose not,' she repeated, staring at the villa with troubled eyes.

'Do you like the house?' he asked casually, his arm around her waist.

'Of course,' she shrugged. 'It's beautiful.' The place was, indeed, sumptuously elegant, modern and stylish in a way that only a great deal of taste and wealth could have achieved. And Leonardo, she had to admit, possessed taste.

'I bought this house with the first really substantial profits that Cressida made. It cost me almost everything I had earned up to that point. But I needed it.'

'Needed?' She raised her eyebrows inquisitively. 'How do you mean, you needed it?'

'I needed the stability. I had a kind of hunger in me for land, for a house, something solid in the world.' He pulled her close, long lashes lowered over those electric eyes. 'Maybe that was the result of losing my parents at a young age.'

She was at a loss for words. She wanted badly to know about him, yet she was also afraid of what she might find out. Would she be able to keep up her defences once she'd learned to see him as a human being, with human feelings and impulses?

The question came out more bluntly than she'd intended. 'How—how did you lose your parents?'

'An accident,' he said briefly.

'What kind of accident?' she pressed.

'An accident of destiny,' he said calmly.

'Why don't you like to talk about it? What kind of accident is an accident of destiny?'

'Curiosity killed the cat,' he reminded her gently.

She wasn't going to be put off. 'Were they killed in a car? A boat?'

'They were killed by a man,' he replied, his voice rough. Despite herself, she flinched.

'You—you mean they were murdered?' she gasped.

'In a sense,' he nodded, 'yes. They were murdered.'

'By whom?' she asked, a cold chill settling in her stomach. 'Was he ever caught?'

'He was above the law.' The smile he gave her was more a grimace of pain. 'Let's go back to the villa. I think we should abandon this topic, Sabrina.'

They walked back to the house in silence, Sabrina's mind working furiously. Abandon the topic? Now that she had finally got behind that rock-like façade to something real beneath? She couldn't.

'I can't get over it,' she said as they walked into the drawing-room, closing the french doors on the evening chill. 'Is this—this person still alive?'

'Now tell me,' he said gently, 'what makes you pursue this subject, Sabrina? You can see that I don't wish to speak about it.'

Sabrina walked to the sideboard. She had caught sight of a photograph in a gold frame, standing between two porcelain pot-pourri. She picked it up, for some reason feeling her chill deepen.

A handsome man with a moustache, cradling a little boy between his knees. On holiday somewhere. In the background, an attractive young woman was waving a bottle of wine gaily. The fashions were those of twenty years ago, and the little boy, gazing with adoring eyes up at his father, was obviously Leo.

'Your parents?'

'That was a holiday we took in Cornwall,' he nodded. His eyes lost their focus for a second, a smile touching his lips. 'My mother was English—you can see her in the background with the wine-bottle. We used to go there often. It was a lovely spot, quiet and peaceful . . .'

She stared at him, this strange new husband of hers. Over the past few days, for the first time, she was seeing him not as a dangerous and incomprehensible enemy, but as a man. A man who, like her, had known grief in childhood.

'Tell me how they died,' she said, watching him intently.

There was ice in his smile. 'Simon Westlake destroyed them.'

CHAPTER FIVE

SHOCK froze her, her blood congealing. The photograph slid through her fingers, its glass cracking as it hit the table. Her face was pearl-white.

'What do you mean?' she whispered, her throat tight and dry.

He laughed, a short, humourless bark. 'You don't really want to know, do you?'

'Of course I want to know,' watching him with fascinated horror, praying this was some cruel joke. 'That's a terrible thing to say, Leo!'

'A terrible act,' he retorted drily. Seemingly with an effort, his face relaxed. He rose, came over to where she was standing, and lifted the cracked photograph from the table. He stared at it with dark eyes for a second, then replaced it. 'Forget it, Sabrina,' he commanded, his finger biting into the flesh of her arm, 'let's go in to dinner.'

'You don't imagine I could eat dinner after what you've just said?' she replied, her voice trembling. Her whole body seemed to be clenched with tension. 'Leo, for God's sake, what did you mean when you said that my father had destroyed them? My father may have been a hard businessman, but he was no murderer——'

'Wasn't he?' The controlled anger in his face frightened her. Again, he visibly forced the emotion down, and took a deep breath. 'I've told you to forget what I said,' he told her. 'I don't wish to rake over this matter tonight.'

'For God's *sake*,' she snapped, close to breaking point, 'how can you do this to me? You can't calmly accuse my father of murder, and then tell me to forget about it. I'm his daughter!'

'Quite,' he said coldly. 'You are his daughter. But now you are my wife.'

'I'm Simon Westlake's daughter first,' she said, almost hysterically. It was the wrong thing to say. His brows came down like thunder over his piercing eyes.

'What do you want, then?'

'Tell me what happened,' she commanded. 'What you meant.'

'Your father simply wanted my father's business,' he told her, his voice like a lash. 'My father was too successful. He got in Simon Westlake's way. I'm sure you're familiar with your father's way of doing things,' he added, the irony in his deep voice making her flinch. 'First he tried to buy my father out. And when that didn't work, he smashed the company—using tactics very similar to those I employed against Westlake over the past few months. My father fought valiantly.' He drank from his glass, the whiteness around the corners of his mouth the only sign of the emotion he was feeling. 'But your father had attacked like a wolf in the night, and it was too late. My father's business crumbled slowly, then broke. In the end, there were only debts left. We had to sell our house, the boat—everything. Your esteemed father,' he said, bowing to her with a deadly smile, 'had the victory.'

'That's a horrible story.'

'The story goes on,' he said gently. 'You look pale, my dear wife. Perhaps you'd better have a whisky.' The glass shook in her fingers as he poured the measure in, but she was glad of the fierce warmth which it spread through her aching heart.

'My father was an obstinate man,' Leo continued, studying the portrait with reflective eyes for a few seconds before laying it down. 'He would not accept defeat. And there were many people who still had faith in him—despite what your father and his tactics had done to him. He began to rebuild, more daringly than ever before, with more advanced designs, more progressive technology. This time, he was sure that there was nothing Simon Westlake could do to him. No one could compete with the brilliance of his designs—a brilliance which was only recognised after his death. He believed that within a few months the whole world would be using components designed by Corleone l'Aquila.'

She watched him in fascinated horror, dreading what she was about to hear.

'What happened?' she asked in a low voice.

'There was a fire. At the research laboratories my father was using in London. Oh,' he said, waving away her question, 'there was no question of an accident. It was arson. Your father had already threatened to do something of the sort. He was utterly without scruples. A sophisticated fire-bomb was planted in one of the ventilator shafts. Plans, experiments, precious designs, all were destroyed. The blaze was hot enough to melt the zinc roof, Sabrina. I saw the molten metal pouring on to the ground.' He picked up the picture again, and looked at it with dark eyes. 'The arsonist hadn't reckoned on one thing, though. My mother was my father's secretary, and she had gone to the lab that night to collect the results of an experiment——'

'Oh no!' Sabrina's knuckles flew to her mouth.

'She was in the building when the bomb went off. It took them three days to find her body.'

With a terrible feeling that she was going crazy, Sabrina rose blindly, seeking some way to escape from what she'd just heard. It was unbearable, it couldn't be true! She blundered towards the door, only to be caught in his strong arms.

'Take it easy,' he said harshly. '*Sabrina.*'

She stared at him blankly, as though he were a stranger. For long seconds she couldn't remember who she was, what she was doing here. Then the world steadied around her, leaving the pain bursting in her heart. 'They didn't mean to kill her,' Leo said quietly. 'You must understand that. Simon Westlake wanted my father's plans destroyed—but my mother's presence there, late at night, was a sheer coincidence. You understand that?'

She nodded, trembling. He released her and walked to the window, staring out at the sunset in frozen, remote pain. 'My father didn't shout or cry. He wasn't that sort of man. But it was too

much to bear. A few days afterwards they found
his car at the bottom of a quarry. They said the
local council hadn't put up adequate warning
signs—but I believe my father half-knew it was
there. Half-wanted to die.'

'Oh, Leo,' she murmured. How in God's name
could she comfort him? Her own feeling of guilt
and horror must be as nothing compared to his
grief. She felt desperately sorry for him; it was as
though all antagonism between them had been
wiped out by the sight of his grief.

As if sensing her thoughts somehow, he looked
up with a tight smile. 'I warned you that it was a
painful topic,' he said. She walked uncertainly
towards him, longing to take him in her arms, but
too shy, too inexperienced to know how to give
him solace. He turned away abruptly, rejecting
her compassion, and she let her arms fall to her
side.

'It's all long ago now, almost twenty years ago.
I was sixteen at the time. You were a child of
three. And there,' he said, his face looking
drained and tired, 'you have the connection
between your family and mine.'

'You should have told me this weeks ago,' she
said in a trembling voice. 'Before you married
me.'

'Have I upset you?' he asked, a strain of irony
in his deep voice.

'You know you have,' she replied. She was
seeing Leo in a new light suddenly, as a man who
had suffered, who had lived through darkness
and pain, just as she herself had done. 'What
happened to you—afterwards, I mean?'

'I recovered,' he shrugged brutally. His show of indifference didn't deceive her quick eyes.

'Did you? Why did you try and destroy the Westlake Corporation? Wasn't that an act of revenge against my father?'

'Of course,' he nodded, his mouth set into a grim line. 'I swore many years ago that I would smash Simon Westlake, Sabrina. It took me a long time to build up the weapons to do it. I named my company Cressida, after my dead mother. When it grew in size and power, I realised I had the perfect tool. And soon, very soon, I had my fingers around Simon Westlake's throat.' His face became an austere mask of anger. 'But he died. Damn him, he died before I could complete what I started.' He turned away, his fists clenched in frustration. 'All that work had come to nothing. I had been watching Westlake for months, assessing everything, analysing everything. I was poised to strike exactly at the right moment, in the fatal place—and a tiny clot of blood deprived me of my revenge!'

Sabrina's face twisted in pain. 'Perhaps that was just as well,' she said. 'Revenge on my father wouldn't have brought you happiness, Leo.'

'Don't pontificate,' he snarled, his brows coming down. 'I wanted justice, justice for the deaths of my father and mother.'

She reached out and took his hand between both her own. 'Leo—my father has gone to a greater judge than this world could provide.'

He seemed to relax at the words. 'Yes,' he said slowly, 'you are right.' His eyes turned on her, mysterious and deep grey. 'But life goes on, does it not, *cara mia*? For the living, life goes on.' For some reason, his words struck a chill into her heart. She stared up at him.

'What do you mean?' A horrible thought crossed her mind like a shadow. 'Marrying me wasn't—can't have been—a part of your revenge?'

His expression didn't change. 'How should it be part of my revenge?' he asked. But the silky irony in his voice constricted her heart in fear.

'Did you marry me to complete your vengeance against a dead man?' she breathed. 'Did you turn to me simply because Simon Westlake had escaped you?'

He considered her with cool grey eyes.

'You mean, to humiliate you?' he asked. A slow smile eased chillingly across his lips. 'To break your spirit? To shatter your heart in the name of the man who was your father? That's a thought, *sposa mia*. A very interesting thought.'

She took an involuntary step backwards, her hands coming to her cold cheeks.

'I don't believe it,' she whispered. 'You couldn't be so cruel, so inhuman!'

'Oh?' he asked, sitting with nonchalant grace on the arm of a sofa, and folding his arms. Then why do you think I married you?'

'I—I thought you married me because . . .' She stammered to a halt, her cheeks flaming. 'I thought you married me for desire. Because you wanted me,' she finished on a whisper.

'But I do want you,' he purred. 'I want you very much, Sabrina.'

The realisation was as clear and as sharp as

crystal inside her. 'You want me as your victim,' she said unevenly. 'Not as your wife. You want me in order to hurt me——'

'Don't be so sure of that,' he said, rising. He took her in his arms, his eyes burning down into her own. His body was hard against her. 'The past is the past, and the present is for living. And I've already said once that pain has no part in my plans for you. I intend to give you pleasure, Sabrina. Much pleasure, of many different kinds.' His kiss seemed to burn her lips like a red-hot iron. She struggled away from him in unreasoning fear.

'No! Leave me alone!'

'So?' His eyebrows rose gently, his arms keeping their iron hold on her. 'Doesn't it please you that I—what was the word you used? Desire you?'

'Not like that,' she quavered, now badly upset. 'You can't do this to me!'

'I haven't done anything—yet,' he reminded her drily. His urbane façade didn't fool her now. She was in terrible danger, danger of being destroyed by Leo's need for vengeance, and she had to get away.

'Please,' she begged him, 'you can't hold me responsible, Leo! You don't know how my father made me suffer, all my life! You can't blame me for things he did before I was even old enough to talk——'

'*Basta.*' He cut her off curtly, his voice vibrant with anger. 'You disappoint me, Sabrina. Don't ever get down on your knees before me, girl. That way you will be trampled into the ground.'

'But if you imagine that I can be held responsible for my father's crimes——'

'I don't think any such thing,' he snapped. 'But let me tell you this—you will maintain yourself with dignity in this house, Sabrina. Or you will be eclipsed as you deserve. As surely as your father eclipsed my family—I *will* humiliate and destroy you.'

'No.' With a massive effort, she controlled herself, and faced him with tight lips. 'I'll never let you do that to me, Leonardo l'Aquila. No matter how justified you may think you are. *Never.*' For a moment they faced each other like duellists awaiting the signal to clash. Then Sabrina turned and walked away. In the past few minutes, her whole universe had been turned upside down; and as for the marriage she'd once thought might just work, she now knew that not one shred of hope must live on in her heart. It was all over, for good.

The meal was a strained, silent affair. Her feelings towards him were in wild turmoil. In one sense, she feared him even more, now that she knew why he had married her, that he had taken her as his bride simply to further a revenge against the misdeeds of Simon Westlake. She couldn't escape her feelings of guilt about that, either. Yet in a dark way she could understand the way he felt. After all, his resolution to execute his revenge was not unlike her own resolution never to marry. Perhaps they were too alike. Too alike, that was, ever to feel more than antagonism towards one another.

One thing was sure, though; she would never surrender to him, never bow to his will.

She ate hardly anything, and as soon as she could, she pleaded tiredness. He nodded, glancing at his watch.

'Yes—I must start early tomorrow. I have to see people in Milan in the afternoon. Perhaps it will be best to have an early night.'

'As you please.' She followed him to the bedroom, picked up her nightgown and a blanket, and walked to the door.

'Where are you going?' he enquired softly. She didn't meet his eyes.

'I'm not spending another night with you, Leo. After this, you must understand that I've got to be alone. I'm going to sleep on one of the drawing-room sofas.'

'You really know how to pile on the agony,' he said tiredly. 'I'm not in the mood for stupidity.'

'Nor am I.' Gritting her teeth determinedly, she reached for the doorhandle. He was with her in a stride, his fingers clamping on her wrist. Her effort to escape was in vain; he jerked her to him, so that her soft body slammed into his hard chest.

'You have much to learn—about me and about yourself,' he growled. He cupped her face in his hands and kissed her hard, his lips almost rough against her own. It seemed to sear her lips, his touch dominating her senses. She trembled against him, stunned by the intensity of his kiss. Then he pushed her away, locked the door with a vicious twist, and pulled the key out, tossing it on to his pillow.

'Now,' he said, his face formidable, 'this argument is over.' Her lips still bruised from his kiss, Sabrina stalked into the bathroom.

She was cursing under her breath as she undressed. He was prepared to use force against her, he'd already warned her of that. Why was she so weak with him, though? Why didn't she stand up to him, resist him the way she'd planned to?

There was no answer. Only the knowledge that Leo l'Aquila had an effect on her that no other man had ever had. He seemed able to melt her, able to send a warm weakness invading her limbs with a touch or a glance.

She got stiffly into bed with him, trying to disguise her inner disturbance. Showing him her fear was dangerous, he'd also warned her about that. Instinctively, she knew he was going to take her in his arms—and when he did so, she had to tense herself to hide the way her heart was pounding, the way her body wanted to mould itself against his.

'Let's not fight,' he said softly, his lips warm against her ear. 'We have so much to find out about one another, my love.'

'Don't we already know all we need to know?' she asked bitterly, closing her eyes. 'Or do you intend to violate me because of what my father did to your family?'

'How melodramatic you are,' he smiled, caressing her cheek, making her tremble inside. 'Can't you simply accept this as a token of the way I feel about you?'

And slowly she realised that his caress was no longer soothing—it had become a track of fire against her back. His fingertips trailed lightly over the swell of her hips, up the silken skin of her spine, to the soft swell of her shoulders; and where they touched, his fingers were leaving tiny flames that licked at her senses.

She tried to pull away from him, but his mouth descended firmly on to hers, his tongue parting her lips, then her teeth, forcing her to surrender— and then to respond. Her own tongue touched his clumsily, shyly—yet her untaught response, inexpert as it was, seemed only to inflame him. With a deep, murmured endearment, he slid the soft material of her nightdress over her hips, his hands finding the smooth fire of her flanks.

'Enough,' she said huskily, trying to stop him.

'Enough?' he mocked. 'We shall never have enough of one another, Sabrina fair . . .'

She pushed hard against his hard chest, but the touch of his muscles under the velvety, sun-warmed skin made her shake, and the thrust turned into a rough caress. When he kissed her again it was as though a fire had exploded between them. Her mouth opened to his mastery like a flower in the sun, and his weight slid with effortless power on to her body, crushing her under the dominance of his strength. She could feel the hard muscles of his stomach and thighs pulsing against her, his arms slipping around her shoulders to press her to him ruthlessly.

'Leo——' But the word was neither a plea nor a protest! To her horror, she recognised in her own voice the husky invitation of a desirous woman.

'*Bellissima Sabrina,*' he said, his voice a purr of sheer, feline pleasure as he looked down at her. He leaned back to unfasten the silk cord of her nightdress, and she watched him helplessly through half-shut eyes. Had a devil been especially made to tempt women, he would have possessed the same magnificent, bronzed body as Leo's, the same utterly poised manner, the same intoxicating smile. She could no longer hide her own desire from herself; she wanted him, longed for him, in a way that shamed her. Nor could she bite back her soft gasp as his sure fingers tugged the pretty knots loose, and thrust the cotton aside to reveal the creamy perfection of her body.

'My dear,' he whispered, his eyes delighting in her trembling nakedness, 'how very lovely you are.' There was a rough, deep note in his voice which thrilled her. 'Do all Englishwomen's lips taste like apple-blossom?' He brushed her throat with his lips, inhaling deeply. 'And your skin smells of warm honey . . .'

'Oh, Leo,' she whispered, aching for him. He bent to touch the satin of her nipples with his lips. She whispered his name again as the skin tautened in pleasure. If only she knew that this passion in him was love, and not hate; the two emotions were so thinly divided that the act of love itself could be either a marvellous tribute or a ruthless assault. Was this rape or seduction? She shook her head restlessly, feeling as though her nerves were going to jump out of her skin.

Her voice was half a groan as she broke free of his drowning kiss, digging her nails into the hard power of his shoulders.

'Don't humiliate me like this, Leo—for God's sake!'

'Is this humiliation?' he smiled, as his lips

touched her neck, the hollow of her throat, the delicate skin over her collar-bone and chest, the full, uptilted swell of her breasts.

'It *is*,' she shuddered, 'because I don't wish it.'

'Your body tells me otherwise.' The power of his thighs forced her to surrender, his breath becoming as ragged as hers now. '*Dio, cara,* I want you.' His desire thrust with bone-melting power against hers, and her responding shudder seemed to shake all the locks of her body open, filling her veins with molten gold instead of blood, making her blaze and ache for a fulfilment she had never dreamed of till now.

'And I want you,' she whispered, unable to stop the words from spilling out of her lips, 'I need you so much, Leo.' She ran her hands over the hard muscles of his back, wrestling with her own burning shame. She had sworn never to bow to his will, never to surrender. Ah, yes, but that had been long, long before she knew what power was his, what sweet torments he could inflict! And he needed her! She had seen the desire naked in his face and in his body! He wanted her—and surely that was enough?

'No,' she whispered, 'no, it isn't enough.'

'What are you saying?' he asked, smiling down at her.

'Please let me go,' she begged, and her eyes were suddenly wet.

Leo's smile faded, to be replaced with a weary grimace. 'More tears? What is it now?'

'This isn't the way to get your revenge,' she whispered. 'You're just becoming another Simon Westlake!'

Anger sparked in his dark eyes. 'What the hell do you mean?'

'It's true, Leo,' she said shakily. 'This is exactly the sort of thing he would have done. But for my sake, for your own sake, don't! I know how badly he hurt you, but you've been corrupted by his example——'

He rolled away, his face pale. 'You've said enough,' he snarled. 'Keep the rest.'

'Please, Leo,' she implored, desperate to get through to him, 'this marriage was begun in hatred and vengeance—don't let it end that way. Perhaps there's a chance that in time we can be friends——'

'I did *not* marry you to be friends with you.' The anger made his mouth a hard white line. He lay back on the golden-yellow sheets. 'But I'm beginning to feel you may be right, Sabrina. Perhaps I never should have married you at all.'

'Oh, Leo.' Heartbroken, she reached to touch his face. 'You make me feel things I never dreamed to feel, you make me need you so badly. But my father——'

'I think we've had enough about your father for one night,' he retorted sharply, brushing her hand away.

'But you don't even try to understand,' she said angrily. 'I know what my father was——'

'God damn and blast your father to the bottom of hell,' he snarled.

'He may be there already,' she shot back, bitterly hurt by his rejection of her, 'but I'm not responsible for his actions, and I never have been!'

'I never said you were.'

'You implied it! Your every action implies it!'
They stared at one another in mutual antagonism
for a second. How swiftly they'd plunged from
the warmth of their love-making to this bitter-
cold dislike!

'I'm tired,' he said shortly. He reached a hand,
and swept out the light.

They both lay tense and angry in the darkness,
waiting for the long night to pass away.

When she awoke in the morning's soft light, Leo
had already left for Milan. She lay among the
tumbled bedclothes, missing him, and filled with
a deep ache.

One myth had been dispelled last night,
anyway. She was no longer indifferent to Leo.
She probably never had been. She wanted him as
a lover, needed him as a man. No one else had
touched her like that before, and no one had ever
broken through the cool barriers she'd put
around herself. Above all, she wanted to get close
to him, and enter the private circle of his
confidence. She wanted to see the laughter in his
eyes, restore the tenderness she'd seen such
tantalising glimpses of.

But Simon Westlake's debts were deeper and
harder to pay than she had ever imagined. And
she had inherited those debts.

She rolled restlessly into the warm trough
where Leo's body had lain. The thought that her
father had destroyed his family twisted in her
heart like a knife. Did he hate her or not? He was
so complicated, so hard to penetrate. But

somehow she had to convince him that she was different from her father, that she understood his pain. That, like him, she had suffered.

She got up and drew the curtains. It was impossible not to feel a lift of the heart as she looked down on to the cypress-lined white marble balustrade, the silvery sea beyond.

As if by some telepathy, Maria, the smiling maid brought a tray of coffee into the room. Her brown eyes were alight with amusement as they took in Sabrina's tumbled hair and unfastened nightgown, and she fastened the cord hastily, flushing.

'Thank you,' she said.

'*Prego, Signora l'Aquila.*' The look on Maria's face made it clear that she thought Sabrina and her master had spent the night in passionate love-making—and, as she curtseyed her way out of the room, Sabrina was sure she was going to relay this information to the other servants.

The irony of it made her smile.

Shaking the dark, scented clouds of her hair into some order, she began her breakfast. Ah, that agonising moment last night . . . Telling Leo he was behaving like Simon Westlake hadn't been exactly diplomatic, but she'd been desperate to stop him. It was so hard to think of him being hurt by anything. He was so strong, so hard.

Last night had shaken her, down to her very foundations. And thinking about her father this morning had brought another thought into her mind, a thought which she had always been too afraid to consider too deeply.

That her childhood experiences had twisted

her character, poisoning her attitude towards men. Even towards sex itself. She had never intended to marry, never intended to have children—and yet such nun-like ambitions were, she knew deep down inside, sterile. Was she, like the Virgin Queen, secretly afraid of a full emotional relationship with a man?

She sipped her coffee slowly, her mind filled with thoughts she had never faced up to before.

And Leo? They were alike in many ways. Two people conditioned by experience and suffering to see the world as a battlefield, conditioned to be cold, unforgiving, unwilling to face emotion. Yet Leo had faced up to emotional involvement, far better than she had. There had been passion in his eyes—not just sensual desire, but a real willingness to *feel*, a willingness almost—almost to love.

The word sent a shudder down her soul. If only she could believe that! Yet she was like a delicate mare that had been badly treated, continually flinching away from expected blows.

She could not answer her own questions. It was impossible to say whether this strange marriage of theirs was going to be a Heaven or Hell. The only thing she could be sure about was that it would be nothing in between. Leo was not a person who leaned towards mediocrity. And nor was she.

She'd just finished dressing when Sara Schiaparelli arrived, dark and very elegant in dove-grey.

'Good morning, *cara*.' Sabrina wasn't expecting the kiss on her cheek; Italian warmth always came as a surprise. 'Leo said you might be at a loose end this morning. I'm going shopping, and I thought you might like to look around. There are some rather charming little boutiques in the village.'

'I'd love to!' Grateful for the thought, Sabrina got herself ready. When she picked her leather bag off the dressing-table, a white envelope tucked just inside the flap fell out. She opened it, puzzled. The crisp banknotes inside were foreign to her, but it was evidently an astronomical sum of money. There was also a note. A very brief one.

Have fun.

She couldn't stop the smile from curling across her mouth. After her recent dark thoughts about him, this had come like a ray of sunshine. How typically practical of him. There was a vein of sweetness in his nature which could warm her deeply.

Talking happily, they made their way down to Sara's primrose-yellow Porsche. Sabrina glanced up at the house as Sara opened the door.

'Your husband has good taste,' Sara smiled, following her gaze.

'Yes,' she said quietly. The place was a jewel, set in a beautiful garden where myriads of roses were still blossoming. The white marble of the villa had been a perfect, though surely incredibly costly, choice for the site, and the orange Mediterranean tiles of the roof made a warm, sunburnt contrast to the coolness of the glowing white stone.

'Did you know that Leo designed and built this house?'

Sabrina shook her head in surprise. 'No, I didn't.' It was the reflection of a mind that loved beauty, a mind more attractive than Sabrina had wanted to believe Leo had.

As Sara had promised, the clothes in the shops were exquisite. The cut of the garments was so obviously Italian, so unlike the styles she was used to. She was going to have to start integrating this ultra-chic styling into her own wardrobe. But she resisted the temptation to spend the vast sums she could so easily have lavished, and contented herself with a pair of black leather high-heeled shoes which looked fabulous on her slim legs.

At noon they had coffee in a little trattoria. Sabrina was growing fond of Sara Schiaparelli. She had a lively, sometimes sharp wit, and beneath her vivacity was obviously a sincere, affectionate person. She admitted candidly that she'd once had more than 'a heavy crush' on Leo.

'But then,' she shrugged, 'so has every woman who's ever known Leo.' Sabrina's expression must have betrayed her, because Sara suddenly patted her hand with an apologetic smile. 'There, I didn't mean to alarm you. There are always females hanging around Leo, but it doesn't mean a thing. He's crazy about you, Sabrina, that's obvious.'

'You think so?' Sabrina said doubtfully.

'*Santa Maria!* You ought to know—you're his wife!'

'I know so little about him,' Sabrina sighed. The coffee was strong enough to be gritty, but it was delicious.

'Contrary to popular opinion, Italian husbands are very loyal,' Sara assured her. 'And if I ever saw a man in love, that man is Leo. At dinner the other night he couldn't take his eyes off you.'

'Couldn't he?' Sabrina asked hopefully. Sara shook her head in mock-resignation.

'How unsure you are. Have you looked in the mirror lately? You've got the kind of beauty that turns men's heads, Sabrina l'Aquila! You don't think Leo would ever be unfaithful to you when you could have any man you wanted just by raising an eyebrow?'

'Oh, nonsense,' Sabrina smiled, grateful for the remark none the less.

'But it's true,' Sara protested. 'Haven't you noticed every man on the island staring after you this morning? You are an object of desire, and you'd better get used to it!' She drained her cup, and put it down firmly. 'Now. A pair of shoes is a poor show for a morning's shopping, *cara*. Did you know that your husband is one of the richest men around? Let's go and spend some of his money!'

CHAPTER SIX

THEY drove back to the villa at two-thirty, both starving. Even after her months at Winfields, Sabrina had to repress her natural instinct to make them a snack, and instead ask Dalila to make a light meal.

The telephone rang while they were eating, and without thinking, Sabrina picked up the receiver.

'Sabrina?' It was Leo's deep voice. 'My agent in Naples has just called to say that your horses have arrived on Capri.

'My horses!'

'I thought that would please you,' he said drily. 'Lorenzo at the dock is having them sent up to the villa. You'll be on hand to take delivery?'

'Of course,' she said eagerly. 'Are they all right?'

'Apparently. They ought to be. I had them put on one of my own air-freighters out of Heathrow, with a top crew.'

'That was very kind of you,' she said awkwardly.

'And I asked one of my best managers to fly with them to Milan.' She could hear amusement in his voice. 'I didn't think anything could surprise Miles Courtnay—but having to shepherd three thoroughbreds to Italy did.'

'Thank you, Leo,' she said softly, moved by

the efforts he had taken on her behalf. Sara smiled knowingly at her tone, and Sabrina felt herself flush slightly.

'I know how much your four-legged friends mean to you. There are stables down past the swimming-pool. They may be a little damp, but I've asked the boy to clean them out. And don't go *anywhere* near the cliffs. Okay?'

'Okay.' She could see his face so vividly in her mind. His voice over the telephone was incredibly attractive, warm and sexy and caring. For some odd reason, it made her feel deeply secure and protected.

'Are you all right?' he went on. 'We didn't part on—er—the best of terms.'

'I'm fine,' she said huskily.

'We'll try again sometime, shall we?' he said in a gentle voice.

'Maybe,' she said in confusion. 'I don't know.' Her face was scarlet, and Sara was openly laughing at her.

'Go on,' Sara called from the table, 'tell him you love him.'

'I can feel your blushes down the line,' Leo said with that soft laugh that somehow wrapped warm arms around her. 'I take it Sara Schiaparelli's there?'

'Yes.'

'Give her my regards. You looked so delicious as I was leaving this morning that I nearly woke you up. But I didn't have the heart to take advantage of a half-awake woman.'

'Good,' she said, feeling ridiculous.

'Enjoy yourself till I get back. I have to go—

I've kept my directors waiting for ten minutes already.'

'Thanks for calling, Leo,' she said impulsively. 'It was good to hear your voice.'

'See you tonight.'

'I'll be waiting,' she replied in a small voice, astounded at her own reaction. She really wanted to see him, wanted badly to be near him. Was it just in reaction to his admittedly beautiful voice that she now felt warm and liquid inside, as though she had been intimately caressed? Or was she beginning to fall in love with this strange husband of hers?

'What cool creatures you English are,' Sara said as Sabrina came back to the table, her appetite gone. 'No one would think you were newlyweds. I trust all that coolness evaporates in the *boudoir*?'

The arrival of three horse-boxes on the driveway saved her from answering, and she ran out to meet them in delight. The horses were nervous as they emerged on to the gravel, but they had evidently been expertly looked after, and her heart went out to Leo again.

'Come for a ride,' Sabrina begged Sara. 'I can't wait to get into the saddle again!'

Sara shook her head. 'I like Porsches, not horses. You go ahead, *cara*. I'll get back home. Will you and Leo come for dinner with us on Friday?'

'Love to,' Sabrina nodded with a smile. 'I'll check with Leo. And thanks for taking me out, Sara. You've been more than kind.'

'I hope we're going to be friends.' The brown

eyes were warm. 'Don't ride anywhere near the cliffs, by the way.' This time Sabrina gave the kiss in return. '*Ciao*.' And the yellow Porsche rumbled down the drive.

As soon as she'd organised stabling for the other two horses with the young groom, she saddled up Criterion, and clambered up on to his back. The big stallion was likely still unsettled, but she was yearning for a ride. no matter how brief, down to the beach.

It was a keen delight to feel his back beneath her, the wind in her hair. The path down was a steep slope, running several hundred yards through trees down to the white sand. There was one uncomfortable place on the way, a strip where a grove of impenetrable cypresses had crept dangerously close to the cliff-edge. The trees forced her to guide the horse within a few yards of the edge, and she leaned forward against his neck, shielding his eye with her hand to try and prevent him from catching a glimpse of the long, dizzy drop to the sea below. The passage was brief but unpleasant—but once they were past the bad part, she let him break into a canter again, and soon they were on the beach.

There was almost no one there, and the long sweep of honey-white sand was clean and empty. Exhilarated, she urged the horse into a gallop, and he responded valiantly, his breath surging into his big lungs as his hooves drummed with muffled beats into the sand.

Today was a new start, a new beginning for both her and Leo. A sudden flash of memory came into her mind—his naked, glorious body, his lips on hers, his hands caressing her flinching skin—and she could not stop the deep shudder of voluptuous pleasure that contracted her stomach-muscles, made her gasp and clench her hands on the reins. Shocked, she kicked the horse into a startled gallop, determined to ride the erotic image out of her veins, where it had begun to take fire.

No—it would not do to underestimate him, either. She recalled one of her first impressions of him, of his potent masculinity. Leo was a real man. And whether she liked it or not, he was apparently intent on making her a woman.

But there was also cruelty just beneath his urbane manner, always ready with sharp claws to strike, wound, revenge. Just because they had shared a few affectionate moments during a long-distance 'phone-call didn't mean that Leo was suddenly going to turn into an angel.

And the more she gave to Leo, the more he would have to hurt her with. If his plan was to take a firm grasp on her heart before tearing it out, she was already dangerously committed to him.

But as she walked the horse up the slope, she was deep in thought. Sara's remark about her coolness had struck a chord in her. Maybe she did seem cold and stiff to other people. Almost no one knew how and where Patricia Westlake and Sabrina had lived all those long years, or who knew the extent to which they had suffered.

After her accession to the Westlake throne, she'd suddenly become the focus of much media attention. She'd been unable to respond to the merciless white light of publicity as a less thin-skinned woman might have done. In the aftermath of her father's death, and the shock of discovering herself to be the new head of Westlake, she'd wanted privacy badly. The ceaseless attention that reporters started paying her had become almost frightening.

It had been a rebuffed tabloid reporter who'd gone back to Fleet Street in disgruntlement one day, and come up with the Ice Maiden legend. It had been a shallow, spiteful article, totally remote from any appreciation of Sabrina's true character; but the large photograph that had accompanied it had burned the image into the public conscious-ness; that exquisite, disdainful face had perfectly fitted the reporter's description of a female Simon Westlake, beautiful and ruthless, who was going to treat the City even more harshly than her father had done. That article had been taken as gospel by thousands of people, even those who should have known a lot better—and like it or not, Sabrina had been stuck with the association.

No, she had never been able to smile for the press, to take off her mask for the world. She had stared icily back at their cameras, not giving a damn what they thought or wrote about her.

Perhaps everyone, barring a very few intimate friends, who would never have spoken to the press about her, thought exactly the same of her?

As she approached the narrow track along the edge of the cliff, she glanced down at the drop visible just next to Criterion's hooves. God, it was a long way down! The sea crawled white several hundred yards down a sheer, basalt-black drop. In the quiet air, seagulls drifted and hovered. Once again, she made her left hand a temporary blinker for the horse, worried that if he saw the sheer drop, he would panic and bolt.

She gasped as the horse suddenly stumbled, and looked down in horror to see his hoof thrusting at the crumbling soil. The edge was coming away! As Criterion jerked forward in alarm, a cluster of loose pebbles and dislodged rocks rattled over the edge, and plummeted swiftly down the gaping drop. Her own heart thumping painfully, she tried to soothe the startled animal. There were still several yards of the narrow path left to go.

Again, he tripped, sending a spray of loose soil tumbling into the void. She clucked soothingly, patting his shuddering neck.

'Take it easy, boy.' But the big horse had made his own mind up, and he spurted the last few yards, jolting her with heart-stopping suddenness, the loose rock crashing and slithering around his heels.

As he cantered on to the solidity of safe ground, he was covered in a sudden lather of fear—and Sabrina turned back in the saddle to study the clifftop walk. The dark cypresses looking over the spot suddenly lent it a sinister air. God—what a sight that would have been—woman and horse tumbling head-over-heels into the chasm, dwindling in the spray-filled air, plummeting into the calm blue sea! She shuddered, and let Criterion have his head back to the house.

She bathed and dressed carefully for Leo's

return, wearing the white cotton voile blouse she'd bought with Sara that day and a skirt of ivory silk she'd made some months back. The open, lacy collar of the blouse emphasised her slender neck and the poise of her head. It was a change to buy clothes instead of making them, especially clothes as nice as this! The pearls her mother had given her went well with the virginal purity of the colours and the rustling, peaceful textures. The effect as she surveyed herself in the mirror in the butter-yellow bedroom was almost bridal—classical, graceful, pristine.

She had discussed the dinner carefully with Dalila, and as she waited for Leo in the sitting-room she was eager for his arrival—and his approval.

Her heart was beating faster as she heard Leo's deep voice in the hall, talking to one of the servants. He sounded angry, and her heart sank. She hoped he wasn't going to be in a savage mood tonight of all nights. But it seemed her hopes were to be dashed, for the end of the conversation was a burst of anger from Leo, and a few miserable apologetic phrases from the servant. Maybe things had gone badly in Milan?

She was pouring a soothing whisky out as he came into the room. Her stomach flipped over. He was clearly angry, his eyes dark and forbidding.

'Will this help?' she smiled, offering him the glass. He knocked it out of her hand with an angry gesture, and took her arms in a grip that made her gasp.

'Little fool,' he rasped, 'what is the meaning of this latest insanity?'

'I don't know what you're talking about,' she said in bewilderment. 'What insanity?'

'Taking your damned horse along the edge of the cliff,' he snarled. 'Didn't I tell you not to do that? Are you blind? Couldn't you see that it was dangerous—deadly dangerous?'

'I thought it was safe,' she protested stiffly. 'Let me go, Leo, you're hurting me——'

'I mean to hurt you,' he snapped. 'You're not safe to be let out alone, it seems.' He thrust her back, so that she sat down heavily on the sofa. 'You will *never* go near that walk again,' he said grimly. 'And that's an order!'

'I shall go where I please,' she retorted, getting up angrily, two spots of vivid colour in her cheeks. After all her preparations, to be greeted with this! 'You can't tell me where to take my own horses!'

'Can I not?' He pointed a finger at her, his eyes merciless. 'If I ever hear that you have ridden your damned horses near that cliff again, I'll have all three of them shot.'

'You wouldn't *dare*,' she gasped, raging at his icy harshness.

'If you love your precious animals,' he snapped, 'don't try and prove otherwise—because I mean what I say.' He bit his anger down with a visible effort. 'You will learn, in time, that I mean everything I say.' He picked up the discarded glass, and rapped it down on to the table. 'Pour me another whisky, Sabrina. And call the maid to clear up that mess.'

'Do it yourself, damn you,' she retorted, shaking with passion. 'If you touch any of the horses, Leo, I'll——'

'I don't care a damn about your horses,' he cut in sharply. 'You are my only concern. And if ever I hear that you've ridden along the cliff-edge, I will destroy them.' He shot her a piercing glance, 'And I'll probably horse-whip you for good measure.'

'Oh, brave,' she sneered, slopping whisky into his glass with a shaking hand, and thrusting it at him, 'kill three horses and whip a defenceless woman—mere amusement for Leonardo l'Aquila, no doubt!' He gulped at the amber liquid, his eyes closing tiredly. 'I suppose you're going to set that poor boy as a spy over me, to make sure I follow your dictatorial instructions to the letter?'

'The groom? He will never work for me again.'

'You mean—you've sacked him?' she asked in disbelief.

'The boy was a fool to let you go riding along that cliff-edge,' he said shortly. 'If you'd fallen I would have thrown him after you.'

She stared at him thunderstruck. His calm arrogance stunned her. She recalled the groom's innocent young face, the rather childish brown eyes and ready smile.

'Leo, you're a callous man,' she said quietly. 'You think you can mess people's lives up, do with them what you please—that poor child couldn't have stopped me! How was it his fault?'

'He should have ridden after you as soon as he saw you approaching that narrow path. He's lived here all his life. He knows those cliffs—you don't.

That place is notorious.' He looked up to her sharply. 'Those who work for me and mine must give me their utter loyalty,' he said coldly. 'I will permit nothing else.'

'And what does your lordship give them in return, pray?' she jeered.

'I give them my utter loyalty in return,' he said looking at her with level eyes, and she dropped her gaze. 'Do you think there is a single member of staff here who would not give his or her life for you, Sabrina? This is Capri, not cold-blooded England, where everything runs according to schedules and regulations. Here we take more account of life and honour.' He tossed the last of his drink back as Dalila peered through the door, her face pale, to announce nervously that dinner was ready.

Leo rose, a formidable and magnificent figure. As if sensing her inner fury, he tilted her chin up to stare at her with cruel, implacable eyes. 'Don't even think of defying me, Sabrina,' he said with steely calm. 'Remember what I've said.' Ignoring her sullen face, he took her arm, and walked her to the dining-room. 'When we have children,' he said more gently, 'I'm going to fence that cliff off completely.'

'Children?' she repeated. In the light of what had just passed, the word struck a chill through her heart.

'Don't look so amazed,' he said drily. 'People do have them, Sabrina.'

'Not people like us,' she said in a low voice. 'I swore a long time ago that I would never subject any child of mine to what I went through.'

He stopped by a massive bowl of roses, and turned her to face him. 'Can you really envisage a future without children?' he asked softly, taking her hands.

'Easily!' Her nerves were on edge with the chord he had disturbed in her. She would never consent to bring another soul into this world to be tormented and oppressed by its parents' cruelty! 'I agreed to marry you, Leo—but I'll never bear your child. I swear it!'

His eyes turned stormy. 'Sabrina,' he said quietly, 'I've made many allowances for your high spirits, your ungoverned temper, your childish passions and spites. Don't push it too far.'

'I see,' she nodded, her heart pounding in her throat. 'Is this part of your appetite for vengeance, then?'

'Vengeance?' His mouth tightened. 'What do you mean?'

'I mean that you need to hurt me,' she retorted, horribly sure that she was right about him. 'You want to humiliate me, degrade me to the uttermost.'

'Do you call bearing my child a degradation?' he said, almost in disbelief.

'Don't be so pious,' she sneered bitterly. 'What else would it be—to make me bear the child of a man I hate? It would be calculated brutality, and you know it.'

He stared at her for long seconds, his eyes seeming to lose their focus. Then he released her wrists and turned away.

'So,' he said, his voice dry, 'that's what you think of me.'

Sabrina didn't answer. Had she gone too far, a long way too far?

'I'm sorry,' she said stiffly, sounding anything but. 'But that's the way I feel.'

'Very well.' His eyes were wintry, lifeless. 'I won't bring the subject up again.' He glanced at his watch. 'I'm not hungry, Sabrina. I'm going to work in my study.' He walked down the corridor, not turning back. Sabrina sagged against the wall, feeling ill with tension.

'*Signora?*' Dalila was watching her in concern.

'I'm sorry,' Sabrina sighed, pushing her hair away from her face. 'We won't want dinner after all, Dalila. Will it keep until tomorrow?'

There was no question in the housekeeper's face. 'Of course, *Signora.* Can I get you something? The wine is open already. Would you like a glass of it, perhaps?'

'I'll take the bottle,' Sabrina said, moved by a grim impulse. Dalila didn't argue, but disappeared into the kitchen, and reappeared with an opened bottle of Chianti and a glass. 'I'm sorry,' Sabrina said again—and carried both to bed with her, not caring what Dalila thought. She needed something to help her overcome these blues, and wine was as good as anything.

She put on her night-gown, and slid between the covers, inclined to cry from pain and humiliation. What had she said to make him treat her like that? The expression on his face had been so very cold, so utterly without feeling. She couldn't possibly have wounded Leo by what she had said?

She poured herself a glass, gulped it down with a grimace, and poured another. It was impossible to tell. Sometimes she was convinced that Leo didn't have any tender feelings towards her. He had married her either as a kind of trophy, or to punish her. And to make her pregnant, make her bear the child of her enemy, would be the fiendishly subtle climax of his vengeance.

She shuddered at her own dark thoughts, and gulped down the smooth wine, longing for oblivion. How little, how very little she knew about other people's feelings!

The strong wine wasn't long in going to her head. She curled up in maudlin self-pity, cradling the three-quarters-empty bottle, and gave way to tears. Oh, for England! Even the purple-faced director would be a welcome sight right now.

Loneliness made it so much worse. Should she ring Clarissa? Beg her to come and stay? She rejected the thought almost at once. She couldn't inflict this misery on Clarry. Hadn't she already decided that, weeks ago? It wouldn't exactly be a holiday for Clarry to come into this strained atmosphere. She might invite Clarry here, one day. But only if she could do so knowing she could hold her head up in her own home. Only if this war with Leo ever resolved itself into anything like a truce.

Ironic ... Such a short time ago she'd been queen-empress of Westlake, with people dancing attendance on her at every step. Now she was nothing more than Leonardo l'Aquila's chattel.

When she awoke the next morning, nauseous and headachy, she was alone. He hadn't come to her bed.

*   *   *

For the next few days she kept as much out of his way as she could, going for long rides along the beach or across the beautiful hillsides, or exploring the villages in the volcanic Maserati that Leo had casually said was hers to use.

When she'd relayed Sara Schiaparelli's invitation to him, he'd rejected it tersely, so she'd gone on her own to spend an afternoon with Sara at their house, a spectacularly modern Spanish-inspired bungalow that they'd designed themselves. It wasn't easy to keep up the pretence that she and Leo were happily married, especially with the intuitive, sensitive Sara.

But Leo, for his part, seemed as glad to be apart from her, burying himself in his study, and once departing by helicopter for the mainland, and returning late at night. They shared only their evening meal, speaking in monosyllables, if at all, and he left her immediately after each meal.

She did not know whether to be relieved or miserable at the fact that he did not sleep with her again, not the next night, nor the next. She'd slept in the massive yellow room alone—or done as much sleeping as she could in her loneliness and depression.

After the first few days she'd wanted to apologise to him, try and make it all right again. Late at night she'd gone to find him, longing for his touch and his voice. He'd been in his study, sprawled asleep over his desk. There was a half-empty bottle of whisky beside him, papers scattered untidily around him. She'd stared at him unhappily for a long while. Then she'd draped a rug gently over him, and had gone back to bed, to lie awake for hours, staring into the darkness.

The next day a letter from William Cattermole arrived, hoping she was well, and telling her that proceedings to recover the stolen funds from Roderigo were going ahead. 'Your husband's lawyers,' he wrote in his dry way, 'are among the sharpest I've met in a lifetime of Law.' There was also news of Westlake. 'Partnership with Cressida is bringing massive advantages already. Instead of a loss, this quarter's profits look like being up some 3%, and we expect a surge next year. May I take this opportunity to remind you that the next Westlake board-meeting is on the 24th December.'

She folded the letter, wondering idly whether she would attend it. Since coming to Capri, the Corporation and all its business had begun to seem a little unreal to her. Maybe even a little unimportant. It was so easy to leave everything in Leo's competent hands.

The trouble was that she was already so dependent on him that she was utterly lost without him. She'd once vainly imagined that he'd married her because he desired her. Now it was she who desired him! He hadn't touched her for days, and she didn't know how much more of this she could bear.

Friday night was stormy, and she had cried herself to sleep at midnight—when, at last, he came. His weight in the bed stirred her into half-wakefulness, and she turned to him. The soft light showed a stubble of rough beard on his jaw, tired lines round his eyes.

'I couldn't keep away any longer,' he said quietly. He was naked, the lamplight gilding his body. 'Why must we be like cat and dog all the time, Sabrina?'

'I don't want us to be,' she said huskily, aching for him.

He smiled wryly, caressing her satiny mouth with his fingertip. 'You're a wild creature, my love. A wild creature from the wet English woodlands. I thought I could tame you with tenderness. But it seems I was wrong.'

'You're not wrong,' she whispered, rubbing her cheek against his caressing hand. 'I'm just mixed-up, crazy. Sometimes I think such horrible things of you, sometimes I need you so badly . . . I'm not consistent, Leo. I'm a mass of wild contradictions.'

'You have a woman's soul,' he said, as though that explained everything. 'That's why I married you.'

'You are a good man, aren't you?' she asked in a timid, almost child-like voice. 'I mean—you're not evil, full of hate . . .?'

With a panther's fluidity he came to her. She gasped as he straddled her with powerful legs, sitting over her hips like a masterful horseman over a fractious mare. His powerful hands took the delicate material at the neck of her night-gown—and with no effort, ripped the material open down to her hips in one smooth, irresistible stroke.

'Leo——'

Her words were silenced under the merciless fire of his mouth, forcing her lips open, and pouring liquid flame into her thoughts.

'Vixen,' he whispered, his voice thrilling in its husky passion, 'tonight you'll see for yourself what sort of man I am.' He kissed her eyelids passionately. 'Now close your eyes. We're going to pretend we're lovers. Not Leo and Sabrina, full of hatred and anger—but some other couple, three weeks married, full of desire and sweet passion. Yes?' His skin felt like hot silk against her untaught body, his kisses and caresses driving her to the edge of losing her sense, as though he wished to torment her now, punish her for her earlier refusals.

Her mind was in a turmoil, but her body was ready for him as it had never been before, liquid and urgent. When at last he possessed her, she gasped out his name helplessly, her soul filled with him. He held her trembling body close against his, his words sweet and burning against her throat.

Love was a dance. She'd never known that before. A dance of bodies and spirits that allowed complete possession one of another. She was his, utterly—just as he was hers. Her man, her own, his potency thrusting deep towards her womb urging her to a completeness of pleasure that was almost too much to bear. He was unhurried, tantalisingly slow, as though he wanted to find out every corner of her soul, every line of pleasure and desire, and fulfil it to the utmost limit. His discipline, she realised intuitively, allowed her the complete freedom to lose herself, to learn the steps of this marvellous, mind-dazzling dance.

'You're in such a hurry,' he smiled tenderly, slowing her gasping with expert control. 'I want to find out so much more about you, my sweet wife . . .' She found herself stretched on the silken sheet, her body his to explore. His mouth was a sweet torment that found her breasts, their aching tips, the smoothness of her belly, the mystery of her surrendering thighs . . .

And when she thought there was no more, that she had reached the limit of endurance he came back to her, murmuring her name. And now there was no holding back, none of the self-control that had allowed her to learn about love so gently, so deliciously; now his need matched hers, and his body was fierce, demanding response from her every sinew.

And at last the agony of desire was quenched in trembling ecstasy. Like a river flooding its banks, her need was released. They clung together as they tumbled down the fiery waterfall of their mutual passion, plunging deep into the depths, sinking, drowning, drifting into a peace more utterly complete than anything she had ever known . . .

CHAPTER SEVEN

SHE had lost a little weight over the last few weeks, she noted appreciatively as she pulled on jeans and a loose cotton blouse. The face that looked back at her from the bathroom mirror was sparkling with health and beauty. Her bath had been delicious, and through the half-open door the bedroom was bright with the morning sunshine, the butter-yellow colour-scheme turning the wintry light into summer. She brushed her hair happily, feeling as though a personal summer of her own had started deep inside her. She had barely awoken from her slumber as Leo had slipped out of bed early that morning, and she had slept on for another hour and a half.

At the thought of meeting those amused grey eyes this morning, the colour touched her cheeks. Yet how unutterably lovely last night had been, the passionate arabesque of their bodies against the rustling gold of the sheets, the response they'd called forth in each other. She had never guessed it could be like that, could never have known.

Dalila informed her that Leo had gone riding on Criterion. The news made her long to be riding at his side, feeling the wind in her face. But a telephone call forestalled her from going out in search of her husband—Michaela Torino, wanting to come round for some translation help with an English book she was studying. Sabrina had to agree. Michaela arrived half an hour later, her arms full of notes, and they went through the book together over a belated breakfast.

Michaela had already noted Sabrina's happy mood with an inward smile.

'You must have slept well?' she enquired diplomatically as they closed the books afterwards.

'Wonderfully well,' Sabrina said happily, and then felt slightly awkward as she saw the sparkle in the girl's eyes.

'At first I had the impression you were not enjoying Capri. That you were suffering from, how do you call it? House-sickness?'

'Home-sickness,' Sabrina supplied.

'Exactly. You seemed unhappy beneath your beauty—but perhaps the delights of marriage are beginning to compensate for home-sickness?'

'Perhaps,' Sabrina said, wishing Michaela wasn't looking quite so amused and knowing. The delights of marriage indeed! Michaela was scarcely out of adolescence. But it occurred to her that this young student, whose pertness made up for her plainness, was probably infinitely more experienced in the ways of love than she herself.

'What about you?' she asked. 'I suppose you're too fancy-free to think of marriage, Michaela?'

'Certainly,' Michaela nodded. 'I am conducting an in-depth study of the eligible men of Italy,' she said with a grin. 'Like the bee, you know? Sip sip here, sip sip there.'

'Indeed?' Sabrina raised impressed eyebrows.

Michaela was probably a wow with the eligible men of Italy.

'But that sort of thing is not for you,' Michaela said decisively.

'No?'

'Not at all. For you there will be only one man, and you are lucky enough to have found him.' She popped a biscuit into her mouth. 'I envy you more than you know, Sabrina. Are you planning a family yet?'

'No,' Sabrina said emphatically. 'Not—not for some time.' But she couldn't be sure of that. Was there, even now, quickening inside her—Leo's child?

Restlessly, she stood up. 'I can't think where Leo's got to. Let's go and find him.'

'Sure. I didn't offend you with that question?'

'Not at all,' Sabrina smiled.

'We Italians tend to dispense with formality.' As if to prove the point, Michaela tucked her arm affectionately under Sabrina's. 'It must be strange for you.'

'Strange—and very pleasant.' They wandered outside into the cool air of the garden. But the thought that she might be pregnant with Leo's baby disturbed her profoundly. She had been for some time now, in the fullest sense, Leo's wife. She had always thought the first time to be marked by discomfort and embarrassment. Instead, it had been marvellous, an almost incredible experience. But motherhood? No, she'd meant it when she'd said she never wanted children, not ever.

'There he is,' Michaela pointed. Leo was

coming down the hillside, looking windblown
and very fit. The big stallion was very obviously
relishing the control of a man's masterful thighs,
a man's firm hand on the rein. The women
stopped as he rode up to them.

'I borrowed your horse,' he greeted her. 'Hello,
cousin. What a day!' He was magnificent,
towering over them from the stallion's high back.

'He seems to have enjoyed himself, anyway,'
Sabrina said, patting Criterion's neck.

'So did I. And how are you this morning, *sposa
mia*?' he enquired. The glint of dry amusement in
his eyes brought the hot blood to her cheeks.

'Very much as usual,' she replied coolly. He
threw back his head and laughed.

'You see what an Ice Maiden she is,' he told
Michaela. 'Last night she was not so cool!' The
colour stayed high in Sabrina's cheeks, but she
refused obstinately to acknowledge his amusement. He stooped in the saddle, and stretched out
a hand to her.

'Come.'

Without thinking, as she'd done that day back
in England, she took his hand. With a surge of
power, he hoisted her on to the stallion's back,
seating her in front of him, between his thighs.

'This isn't safe, Leo,' she protested, flushing at
Michaela's delighted laughter.

'Yes it is,' he contradicted. 'We'll take
Criterion back to the stables. See you at the
house, Michaela—perhaps we'll go out in the
yacht this afternoon, yes?'

'Oh, *yes*,' Michaela said happily, and ran back
to the house like the colt she was.

His strong arms were around her waist, and he set Criterion moving with a rap of the reins, ignoring her dismay. His chest was hard against her, his mouth against her ear.

'Did I hurt you last night?' he asked in a growling whisper which set her heart quivering. 'Was I too rough?'

'You—you may have been,' she replied as though it were a matter of absolutely no importance. 'I can scarcely remember it, anyway.'

'Damnable woman,' he grinned, 'do you like to see me angry? But I'll tame you yet! Your body tells me the truth, even if your tongue lies to me.' His teeth were sharp on the soft nape of her neck, and she yelped indignantly, making Criterion toss his head.

A new groom was waiting for them at the stables, a bright-eyed boy in his late teens, who greeted them with a disarmingly gap-toothed smile. After the scare of her last outing Sabrina had been too frightened to ride, contenting herself in the weeks that had followed with the occasional visit to the stables to see Criterion, so she had not yet met the new lad.

'This is Enzo,' he informed her as he let her slide to the ground. 'He'll be in charge of your steeds from now on—and he has strict instructions about the cliffs.'

The boy kissed her hand with native good manners. She liked his obvious sturdiness, and the sure way he took the stallion's head to lead him inside the stable—and had to admit that Enzo was an improvement.

As they walked back to the house, his arm tight around her waist, he turned to her.

'I've brought a little present for you.'

'How kind,' she said warily, suspecting some new trick. Her reaction made him grin.

'What a wild thing you are. Don't you trust me?'

They didn't go straight to the long drawing-room, where Michaela was waiting, but stopped in the hall. He took a flat leather case out of a drawer, and presented it to her.

'I bought these for you in Naples yesterday,' he informed her, and waited with fathomless eyes as she prised the box nervously open.

The diamonds blazed on the watered silk, two exquisitely-cut prisms that had captured the sun. Dazzled, she took the earrings into her palm to study them. Each contained one big, first-water stone set on a sunburst of smaller gems. They had been chosen with perfect judgment, she knew. Against her raven hair, the priceless jewels would dazzle like stars.

'Don't you like them?' he asked gently. Damn the man! How did he always manage to get past her defences? Tears prickled behind her eyes, and she kept her head obstinately bowed.

'They're—very nice,' she muttered. But he had caught the catch in her voice.

'*Cara*,' he said in surprise, lifting her face with a hand beneath her chin, 'you're crying!'

'Are these my payment for the last five weeks?' she asked tearfully. He took the jewels from her, and fitted them deftly into her earlobes, his hands warm against her cool cheeks, then turned her to face the mirror behind them. The brilliance of the diamonds set her face off perfectly. His arms came round to clasp her under the breasts, his eyes meeting hers in the mirror.

'Every moment of those weeks have been very precious to me,' he said softly. 'But these are not payment, Sabrina. Just a tribute.'

'I don't deserve them,' she said awkwardly. 'They must have cost a fortune.'

'But you are worth a fortune to me.'

'And these are to mark your conquest of me?' she suggested wryly.

'Perhaps,' he nodded, unperturbed by her acid. 'But not in the way you think.'

'How, then?' she asked, touching the beautiful things in her earlobes.

'You don't give me credit for any tender feelings, do you? You think I'm made of stone. You think I'm like your father.'

'No.' She shook her head. 'I said that to hurt you, but it wasn't true. And I'm sorry I said it.' She met his eyes. 'You're a man who gets his own way. But you don't use force. You have—other methods of persuasion. In exchange for what you take, you give gifts.'

'Such as pleasure?' he murmured, and her flush deepened.

'You know I can't deny that,' she said, her voice low.

'I wanted you very much indeed, Sabrina.' His eyes looked deep into her soul. 'I want you still.' She shuddered, her arms prickling with goose-flesh.

'How *can* you want me? Don't you hate me?'

'Because of your father?' He smiled wryly. 'Has it seemed that way to you?'

'No,' she admitted, looking away.

'Then why is there always this tension between us?' he asked gently. 'It doesn't have to be there, Sabrina.'

'Doesn't it?' She searched his face. 'Sometimes I think we're trapped, both of us. Trapped by who we are, by what happened to our parents——'

'Only your own mind traps you,' he interrupted brusquely. 'You like to imagine that I married you simply to torment you, to humiliate you as part of some crazy vengeance.' He smiled slightly. 'A somewhat weird idea.'

'I might be a shrew, you know,' she said inconsequentially. 'For all you know, I might make your life a misery.'

'Shrews can be tamed,' he reminded her with a glint in his eyes. 'And now let's go down and get the yacht ready.'

The day out in the yacht was among the most memorable she'd spent. She was nothing like as accomplished a sailor as Leo and Michaela were, but by the end of the day she knew she'd never get sailing out of her system. The tautness of full sails, the white hull slicing through the grey waves, the vibration of the teak deck beneath her feet, these were experiences she'd always want to repeat.

Whether out of respect for her exhaustion she didn't know, but Leo didn't make love to her that night. Instead he worked late, and she had already fallen asleep by the time he came to bed. Over breakfast the next morning, he surveyed her flushed cheeks and still-tumbled hair.

'The fresh air does you good, *cara*. You're a sailor born.' He drank his coffee, then dabbed his mouth. She had an odd sense that he was planning something, waiting to spring something on her, and she watched him warily. 'Do you like the opera?' he asked casually.

'I love it,' she replied, surprised, 'Why?'

'Maria Dubarry is singing *La Sonnambula* in Naples tonight. I have a box at the theatre. Shall we go?'

'Oh, yes!' she breathed in delight. 'She's marvellous. I'd love to hear her!'

'Excellent. We'll go across in the helicopter, and have dinner at a restaurant later on. Agreed?'

'Agreed,' she nodded with shining eyes. Opera in Naples—and travelling there by helicopter! She'd wear the midnight-blue dress she'd made some months earlier, she'd decided already. Modelled on an exquisite evening-gown of the 1950s, she had reduced the extravagantly flowing lines to their bare essentials. But she'd kept the opulent pleats to retain that mysterious, alluring quality that was so utterly feminine.

Studying herself in the mirror that evening, she decided that the effect was dramatic—yet also feminine, vulnerable. And somehow, completely different from the Sabrina Westlake who had inherited Simon Westlake's empire a few short months ago. It was not so much that there was a difference in her physical appearance—though her pale cheeks were now tinted with healthy colour—as that her whole bearing was more poised, more mature. Suggesting a capacity for joy that hadn't been there before.

Her thick black lashes scarcely needed mascara, but she used eye-shadow to add sophistication, and a deep rose lipstick to enhance the perfection of her mouth. Her deep black hair gleamed with health, and she brushed it vigorously now, letting its heavy, glossy curls fall in elegant profusion down to her shoulders. The diamond earrings looked dazzling in her ears, completing the picture. Wondering how Leo was going to react to her appearance, she wrapped the sable around her shoulders, and in its dark sensuous folds, walked through to the sitting-room where her husband, who had already dressed, was waiting for her.

His grey eyes drank her in with unmistakable pleasure, and her heart skipped a beat at the expression that crossed his magnificent face.

'You remind me of that time we met outside the Albany,' he said softly, 'in the snow. You looked ravishing then, an ice-queen with frost in your smile.'

'And now?' she asked.

'Now you look like a creature of the summer, waiting for the first buds of spring.' He held her eyes for a long minute. Then the chopping roar of the helicopter announced that it was time to think of departing. 'Come—we mustn't be late.'

Huddled in the rich warmth of her fur, Sabrina pressed herself against Leo as the helicopter rose into the evening sky.

The last glow of a winter sunset was fading

gold and tawny silver in the West, and the sky
above was dark. Thrilled, she stared through the
Perspex bubble at the dark sea below, and the
sparkling lights of Naples on the mainland ahead.
Leo's strong arm was around her as the pilot
swooped the helicopter through the gathering
dusk, and a mixture of nervousness and delight
took hold of her.

'Are you enjoying it?'

'Loving it! I'm beginning to see why you
prefer travelling this way. It's thrilling.'

'Naples.' She followed his pointing finger to
the spider's web of lights that was Naples,
coming up ahead. By night the city was
bewitching, enchanting. It took barely five
minutes to get to the city centre. The helicopter
pilot flew them daringly close above the rooftops,
and Sabrina clung to Leo's arm, almost hypnotised by the beauty of it all.

'Naples has always been my spiritual home,'
Leo told her softly, and in the dim light, she
could see that his eyes were tender as he gazed
down at the brilliant city below. 'Though I was
born in England, and half of me is technically
English—I'm afraid I'm a Neapolitan to my
soul.' He smiled at her. 'And tonight I want to
show you some of Naples' riches.'

The helicopter found an unlikely landing-place
among the domes and castellations of an exquisite
17th century *palazzo* in the centre of the city.
Silent with awe, Sabrina let Leo lead her down
through the building to the lift. Stunned by the
massive marble interiors, the Baroque frescoes
that covered the arched roof, she turned to him.

'What is this building?'

He smiled. 'The Eagle's nest. This is the Cressida building—my headquarters.'

She gaped at him. '*This?* But it's—it's . . .'

'Beautiful? Yes,' he nodded, pausing to look up at a row of marble statues at one end of the entrance hall. 'But the building was badly run down when I bought it. It cost me many millions of *lire* to restore it to its former grandeur. Do you think it was worth it?'

Her shining eyes were all the answer he needed. Amazed by the utter magnificence of the building, Sabrina began to have an idea, for the first time, of the scale and scope of her husband's wealth.

'Yes,' she said, looking with dazzled eyes at the blazing chandelier that hung over the inlaid marble of the entrance, 'you are a Neapolitan to your soul, Leo. Only you could have chosen a Baroque palace as your business headquarters. It's wonderful!'

'Wait until you see the Opera House,' he promised. 'It's a little younger than my Palace, but it has rather more razzmatazz.'

Despite his promise, nothing could have prepared Sabrina for the interior of the Opera House. As they walked through the heavy velvet curtains into their box high above the stage, Sabrina's senses registered only a blaze of crimson and gold. She leaned with Leo over the edge of their little balcony, and drank in the scene with glowing eyes.

For one thing, the theatre was huge. From the sea of people beneath them, a hubbub of conversation and laughter, cigar smoke and expensive perfume, rose to the crenellated ceiling above. The curtains were tantalisingly closed over the stage, emphasising the splendour of the towering proscenium arch.

Red and gold seemed to be the dominant colours. Every conceivable surface in the great theatre had been decorated with gilt stucco or statuary set in recesses. The bowed front of each box was as highly-decorated as the stern of a King's galleon; and indeed, there was something nautical about the place. It was, Sabrina decided, like some bejewelled, magical ship, about to set sail for some unexplored wonderland.

When they sat back in the plush seats, there was a bottle of white Frascati cooling in an ice-bucket behind them and two glasses on a silver tray. Sitting down, they were invisible to the people below, isolated in their luxurious world high above the common herd! But several people came into the box to greet Leo and be introduced to Sabrina. Glad of her elegant dress, Sabrina was able to disguise her shyness in front of the immaculately turned-out Neopolitan society women who came in to meet her with undisguised Southern curiosity in their dark eyes. Poised as ever, Leo introduced her to a succession of people before the lights dimmed, though not a single name stuck in her head. And then the curtain parted on the elaborate stage-scenery, and the real magic of the evening began.

Despite her French surname, Maria Dubarry was a Neapolitan, whose thrilling sweet soprano carried a legendary huskiness that had earned her the title 'the nightingale of Naples'. This audience obviously adored her, and she responded to their adoration by singing with a ravishing sweetness that brought the tears to Sabrina's eyes.

The first act of the opera, a continuous paean of love, was sung with a piercing beauty that seemed to melt her very soul. She found herself leaning against her husband's powerful shoulder, her head against his cheek so that her raven hair caressed his face, her hand clasped in his.

She had always loved opera, but this was a new experience for her. She could never have believed how powerfully the music would affect her. *La Sonnambula* was an opera about love—love in all its manifestations, from the tenderest melancholy to jealous tempests. The thrilling soprano fluttered and swooped against the rich masculine tenor of the male lead, their singing almost a musical lovemaking. The restrained passion reminded Sabrina irresistibly of her own relationship with Leonardo l'Aquila.

As she clung to him in the darkness of their box, her eyes dim with tears, Sabrina reflected how strange and confused her feelings about Leo were. In one sense, she was always running away from him, like a doe running from a huntsman; in another, she longed to be caught, longed for the power in his arms that would crush the resistance out of her, imprison her by his side for ever!

Was it possible—just possible—that she was wrong about Leo?

Could he, after all, feel towards her any of the feelings she held for him? She had for so long

believed that he had trapped her into marrying
him specifically to carry out a savage revenge
against her. Was that true? Could it be true?
Could the man who made love to her in the way
Leo did—the thought of it, even now, brought
her heart up into her throat—could he really hate
her, be waiting only for an opportunity to wound
her?

The end of the first act broke the spell of her
thoughts as the lights went up, and the audience
erupted into thunderous applause, throwing
garlands and bouquets—a foretaste of the con-
clusion—on to the stage. With a long, shuddering
sigh, Sabrina leaned back in her chair, and met
Leo's eyes with a quivering smile . . .

The candlelight in the secluded alcove of the
restaurant made Leo's eyes fathomless, mysterious. And also, she thought in puzzlement, a little
sad.

'I've heard Maria Dubarry sing many times
before,' he said, 'but never so beautifully as
tonight.'

'It was ravishing,' she agreed. 'But . . .' She
hesitated uncomfortably. He smiled, raising one
eyebrow in gentle query.

'But—what?'

'Well, she seems to have made you melancholy.'

For an instant, he seemed about to say
something, and then he shrugged. 'Beautiful
singing is always a little sad, not so? Perhaps it's
my Neopolitan blood. So—tonight we had better
cheer ourselves with good wine.'

'If you say so,' she smiled.

The restaurant he had taken her to after the opera, *La Conca D'Oro*, was famous for its Neapolitan cuisine. The headwaiter had guided them to a candle-lit alcove which discreetly commanded the opulent glitter of the main dining-area, and with the reverence of a high priest, declared that he himself had composed the menu. The food promised to be sumptuous, yet Sabrina had no appetite—and with a woman's quick intuition, she guessed that Leo was feeling the same way, though she could not tell why. Perhaps, she thought, the beauty of Dubarry's singing had keyed them both up.

There was also, she reflected uneasily, a very powerful tension between them tonight—a tension that was half-emotional, half-nervous. Their eyes met again, and she looked away quickly.

'Did you design that dress, too?' he asked, his eyes intent on her gown.

'Yes. I never thought that I'd ever wear it, though.' She smiled nervously. 'It often happens. I design a dress that pleases me, and then I realise I'd never have the courage to wear it.'

'I would have said you thrive on challenge and conflict,' he suggested.

'No, I love peace and quiet. I hate conflict of any kind—it makes me ache inside.'

'Really?' He raised a sceptical eyebrow. 'And yet you've been fighting *me* tooth and nail these two months past.'

She toyed with her food in discomfort. 'I only fight you because you threaten to crush me, Leo,' she said in a low voice. 'I fight for my survival—just as any creature would.'

The arrival of the waiter with a crisp, succulent plate of *frutti di mare*—shellfish and squid fried in batter—prevented him from answering her, and they ate in silence for a few minutes. Then Leo looked up at her, the candles reflecting two yellow flames in the orbs of his eyes.

'Do you still believe I wish to crush you, Sabrina? Have you never learned to trust me?'

If only she could get some reassurance from him, some word of tenderness, some promise that he loved her after all! 'You shouldn't have married me with a pistol to my head.' She smiled wryly at him, hoping what she was saying would wring a statement out of him. 'Your wooing was very aggressive, Leo. That didn't make a very good start—for me, anyway. And I still believe, yes, that you married me, at least in part, because you wanted to torment me. To get some revenge of your own for the death of your parents.'

'No doubt your psychology is accurate.' His smile was made mysterious by the soft shadows cast up from the candle-flames. 'And supposing I did marry you for those reasons, *sposa mia*—would it be impossible for me to change my mind?'

'It's catch-22, isn't it?' she asked. 'Either way, we both lose.' But if only he knew how achingly badly she wanted to believe him! 'Anyway, isn't it a bit late to change your mind?'

'Perhaps it's never too late.'

'But supposing I find I'm unable to change *my* mind?' She met his eyes as directly as she could.

'You held me a hostage for the livelihood of my employees. My consent to this marriage was the ransom needed to free them from the threat of annihilation.'

'Granted,' he said calmly. 'So what?'

'You're being remarkably obtuse for a brilliant man,' she said sadly. 'That's what I shall always remain, Leo. Your hostage. And I shall always feel to you as a prisoner feels towards her jailer.'

There was a long silence, filled with the distant clatter and chatter of the other diners. She held her breath in painful expectation. She'd been cruel, but only to get him to expose his real feelings towards her. Would he tell her the words she so desperately wanted to hear, that he needed her, the way she needed him? The waiter, looking miserably at the barely-touched plates, materialised beside them, and cleared the table for the next course.

When he had gone, Leo leaned back in his chair, his tapered fingers drumming restlessly on the linen.

'Yet you cannot deny that you have responded to me?' he demanded. 'After all, I have felt you in my arms, Sabrina, have looked into your eyes while we made love.'

The flaw in her argument yawned in front of her. 'Sex isn't everything! In fact, it's nothing!'

'It doesn't touch you?' he asked in disbelief.

'Only in a purely physical sense,' she stammered. 'I can't help what my body does—if you were to whip me, I wouldn't be able to stop myself from crying out. Nor can I help myself when——' She faltered again. 'When you make love to me. It's just physical—it doesn't touch my heart. And in my heart, I shall always be a stranger to you.'

She bit her lip as he looked away, the grim set of his authoritative mouth revealing how deeply her words had cut.

'Then there seems very little to be said,' he shrugged, draining his glass. Dully, she knew her little stratagem hadn't worked. 'And what,' he went on casually, 'if I were to offer you your freedom, Sabrina?'

'My freedom? What do you mean?'

'Freedom from me,' he clarified dispassionately. 'Freedom for both of us. What if I were to offer you the divorce you wanted?'

Her heart jolted inside her as though an electric current had passed through her chest. Her throat suddenly dry, she looked at him with stricken eyes.

'I never said I wanted a divorce,' she whispered.

'I'm saying it for you.'

'You—want to divorce me?' She couldn't believe it for long seconds; her lips quivered into a half-smile. 'Are you serious, my love?'

'I am not your love, Sabrina.' His face was as immovable as stone, his eyes hard and cold. 'Nor am I, contrary to what you so devoutly believe, a man who enjoys inflicting pain on others. It gives me no pleasure to feel that my wife hates and fears me. So.' He opened his hand, palm upwards. 'I give you your freedom. And rest assured, your Corporation will be safe. You can go back to running Westlake, and you'll never see or hear from me again.'

Stunned, she looked up at him with white face and staring eyes. 'Do you mean this?' she whispered. The waiter had reappeared, his face nervous, and they were silent as he served up the quail *en casserole* with fresh vegetables. The wine steward was pouring a vintage Burgundy to accompany the food, and Leo tasted it gravely, nodded his approval, and then surveyed Sabrina's pale face as the waiters effaced themselves once more.

'You don't seem very pleased,' he said ironically. 'Isn't this what you've wanted, ever since we left England?'

'Yes,' she whispered again. 'I thought—I thought there was no divorce in Italy?' she faltered.

'There is now,' he said calmly. 'But I propose the Mexican variety. More expensive—but so much quicker. It would barely take a fortnight to arrange.'

'I see,' she said. Her body was trembling in every limb, and an uncontrollable ache was spreading through her chest, as though her heart were literally breaking in half. Through her bewildered and reeling thoughts, one terrible idea was clear. Her idea of exposing his true feelings had worked with a catastrophic vengeance. Leo didn't want her any more. Leo had tired of the game of chasing her and was offering her her liberty.

'So?' he pursued, chewing a mouthful of the succulent quail and raising his eyebrows at her,

'What do you say?' Numb, she picked her knife and fork up, and cut her food. In her mouth it was as tasteless and textureless as cotton-wool. 'Come on—do you accept my offer?' Leo repeated impatiently.

'I—I need time to think,' she pleaded unsteadily. 'Perhaps I've given you the wrong impression——'

'In any case, it doesn't matter,' he said crisply. He paused to sip some ruby wine and savour the bouquet on his palate. She realised with disbelief that the whole thing must mean very little to him. 'A good vintage,' he judged, looking through the wine against the candlelight. He glanced at her taut face again. 'My own mind is made up. This is the end of the road for us. I don't want to go any further, and you've just said that you don't either. We'll fly to Mexico some time next week. A kind of honeymoon in reverse, eh? We'll probably be divorced before the end of the month. You could be back in your beloved Winfields by Christmas.' His grey eyes glittered like cold amethysts. 'Isn't that what you want?'

'Oh, Leo,' she whispered in horror, her throat stiff and aching.

'Excellent,' he commented coolly. 'I'm glad you agree. The farce had gone on too long.'

'Yes,' she said dully, staring at her plate. 'I suppose it had.' The farce had been her own unbelievable arrogance in assuming that he cared a jot for her. That he would put up with her vacillations and sulks for ever.

'Then I'll start organising our divorce tomorrow. Congratulations, Sabrina.'

She looked up at him blindly.

'You've won. Aren't you pleased?' He smiled coldly, raising his glass to her. 'To Reno. And the end of the comedy.'

She raised her glass, and drank the bitter liquid with closed eyes.

How she managed the rest of the meal she could not tell later. Her numbness protected her to an extent, and she sat as though in a dream, ignoring the delicious dishes that were set before her. Leo talked calmly and unconcernedly throughout, apparently utterly indifferent to her pale cheeks and downcast eyes. And all the time she felt as though she were bleeding inside, as though her very life-blood were slowly draining away through some inner wound.

Divorce! Leo no longer wanted her . . . As the thought sank into her mind like a branding-iron into tender flesh, her mental anguish deepened. The irony of it was so very bitter! She had, through her indifference, her cruel words to him, forced him into rejecting her.

And she no longer wanted to be rejected.

Now, for the first time, she realised how vital Leo was to her existence. She could no more do without her husband than she could have done without oxygen or water. And her marriage—the marriage she had spurned and belittled from the first—was the most consumingly important thing that had ever happened to her.

Now she was remembering the thousand moments of tenderness and affection they had known together, the one-ness, the gentleness—

and yes, the love. The love that he had offered her time after time.

The love she had rejected, either because she misunderstood it, or because her own crippled emotions hadn't been capable of responding.

But she wasn't crippled any more! Leo had healed the wounds left by her father, had restored the wings to her heart. She was now a woman, capable of feeling, capable of loving.

And deeply, irrevocably, inextricably in love with Leo.

All destroyed now, all in dust and ashes. She had finally pushed him over the edge; and whatever chance there had once been of his feeling any soft emotion for her was now lost for ever.

She stared at him with yearning eyes, longing to burst out with the truth—that she never wanted to be away from him, that he was the most important thing in the world to her and always would be! If only she could take him by the hands and *tell* him—tell him what he meant to her, that all her protestations and cruelty had been mad folly——

But she couldn't. The words stuck in her throat, as though she were paralysed.

'*Sabrina.*' His steadying hand touched her shoulder, and she realised with a gasp that she had been on the verge of fainting.

'I'm sorry,' she faltered, putting her fingers to her temple, 'it must be the heat—or the wine—'

'Your triumph must have gone to your head,' he observed drily. 'Come—we'll get back to the helicopter, and get you home into bed.' He looked at her pearly-white face, her bloodless lips. 'You're all right?'

'I'm fine,' she whispered.

He shrugged indifferently. Then he signed to the waiter for the bill.

CHAPTER EIGHT

By the time she was undressing in the golden-yellow bedroom, Sabrina was very close to tears. She had been unable to say a word to Leo on the helicopter trip back, and they had travelled in silence for the most part. And this time they had sat apart, not touching, Leo smoking a cigar, something she had never seen him do before, as he stared out of the canopy bubble at the sea below.

As she let the dress slip from her shoulders, she looked into the mirror—to meet Leo's dark eyes on her. Then he turned away, and began unbuttoning his shirt with casual indifference. As soon as he had gone into the bathroom, Sabrina climbed wearily into bed.

But her grief could no longer be restrained, and when Leo climbed into bed with her, her pillow was damp with tears.

When she felt his warm caress on her shoulder, she turned to him, reaching out for him, determined that now she was going to tell him the truth, tell him how much he meant to her.

His mocking smile killed the words on her lips.

'You're very eager tonight, *sposa mia*. I trust this is purely physical—and not going to touch your heart?'

She stared at him in horror. Then despair took her. So be it, then. 'Oh yes, it's purely physical,' she said quietly. 'Have no fear of that, Leo.'

'I'm glad to hear it,' he nodded. 'After all, even people who hate one another are capable of this, not so?'

He took her without preliminaries, as possessively as though she were his slave. The driving need in him was shocking, overwhelming. Her arms were about his neck as his mouth plundered hers, the warm, musky scent of his skin a torment. As her body arched to him, she tore her mind loose from all thoughts, abandoning her pain, her grief, her anger, in the intoxicating closeness of Leo.

This wasn't the gentle love-making of other times. Now he was like a stallion, ruthlessly using her body, imperiously demanding to be used in return. It was almost brutal, a savage physical delight that swept everything aside, making her call out in an ecstasy that was almost pain.

She was dimly aware of the silky sheen of sweat on his bronzed body as he crushed her, his lips hungry against her panting throat, moving to her breasts, his tongue rough against her nipples as he sucked each rose-pink bud to its fullest peak of aching desire. And his own hunger was evident in the unspoken words she could hear rumbling in his throat.

It was over too soon, their bodies shuddering in a violent climax of strained sinews and taut limbs. Then, slowly, painfully, they disentangled themselves, the warm, wet pains of afterlove creeping through the golden haze to bring them back to reality.

'Now,' he murmured in dreamy content, lying back, 'we've said a formal goodbye. You are my hostage no longer . . .'

The pain twisted in her stomach, as fierce and cruel as his love-making had been sweet, and she turned away from him, staring into the darkness with tear-dimmed eyes.

When she awoke out of nightmares, Leo had already left for a business meeting in Sorrento. With her awakening, the first wave of memory hit her. The comedy, as he had drily remarked, was at last over. By rights, this should have been one of the happiest mornings of her life. Not one of the most wretched.

She washed and dressed in a daze, wondering how on earth she could change the situation. Was it too late, even now, to confront Leo—to try and explain to him what a terrible succession of mistakes their marriage had been? But there seemed to be no way she could persuade him that her own fierce reactions to him had not been out of malice or spite, but out of inexperience and fear.

It all seemed so hopeless. Leo would never believe her now. And even if he did believe her, it would make no difference at this stage; by her actions, she had driven every vestige of tenderness out of his heart. He was prepared to use her body—but not to trust her.

As she tugged her sweater on, she thought bitterly that Leonardo l'Aquila's revenge could not have been more complete! Maybe this had been his idea from the start, to make her love him, and then thrust her out of his life forever. He was going to hurt her, yes, and more bitterly than anything in her life had done—but he was going to hurt her in a way she could never have anticipated or guarded against. How ironic, that it should be her love for Leo that would, in the end, be the instrument of her punishment.

She went down to the village in the Maserati, needing badly to talk to Sara Schiaparelli. But the only person at the Spanish villa was the housekeeper. The Schiaparellis were on the mainland, meeting a client. Sabrina sat in her car, feeling despair sweep over her. Who could she turn to? Michaela was sweet, but too young to understand any of the terrible things she was going through. She drove back home in the end, unable to bear the thought that she'd never see Leo again.

He didn't return that night. All she got was a terse phone call saying he was spending the night in Sorrento. He didn't say where or with whom, and left her to spend a lonely night in grief-stricken imaginings.

And when he eventually returned, towards midday the next morning, Sabrina's heart sank even further at the sight of his face. It was grim and set, the passionate mouth compressed to a hard line, the grey eyes cold as winter.

They ate an early lunch in silence, Sabrina glancing at him nervously as she tried to rack her numbed mind for something to say, some speech to make.

'Leo,' she began at last, her voice dry and

faltering, 'about this divorce. I want to say something——'

'Hasn't everything been said?' he interrupted impatiently, his eyebrows coming together in a frown. 'Let's not rehearse the finale any more, please!'

'Everything *hasn't* been said. Not on my part, anyway!'

'I see,' he commented with a weary sigh. 'You mean you've thought up some more poisonous remarks since last night?'

'No——'

'Or perhaps you think we should go out with a bang, and now you want to start a fight?'

'*No*,' she snapped, trying to fight down the hurt resentment his words were provoking in her. 'I don't want to fight you. I want us to have a second chance. I want you to listen to what I have to say.'

'Did you ever listen to what I had to say?' he asked silkily.

'Maybe I never did. But I'm asking you to hear me out this time.'

'It's too late. I've heard you out too many times, Sabrina.' His fingers had began to drum on the tablecloth, a danger-sign she knew of old. 'I telephoned my American lawyers this morning, and asked them to institute divorce proceedings at once.'

Shock clawed at her. She stared at him, the colour draining from her face.

'At once?' she repeated in panic.

'Money works wonders where bureaucracy is concerned. There are various applications to be made, various fees to be paid. But there will be only the minimum of delay, I assure you. We'll be flying out to Mexico as soon as the application is passed. Say in two or three days' time. We might even meet friend Roderigo.'

'I can't bear it to end like this,' she cried out, her eyes flooding with tears.

'What does it matter? You said last night we were strangers. Why should you weep over departing from a stranger?'

'That's a horrible thing to say,' she stammered, 'after what we have been to each other!'

'And what were we?' he asked in a velvet voice, leaning back in his chair to study her as though she were some unique specimen. 'I thought you told me that our love-making was purely physical, and not of the heart?'

'I was lying,' she said in a low voice. This was not her husband talking, the man she'd come to know and love. This was the Leo l'Aquila who'd confronted her in the snow, who'd wanted to destroy Westlake with the scientific efficiency of an exterminator.

'Indeed?' The amused smile held no warmth. 'Please don't tell me you're getting sentimental now that we have to say goodbye?'

'We don't have to say goodbye, Leo! I've been so terribly wrong about a lot of things, ever since the beginning. But so have you. We've misunderstood each other, misjudged each other. For the love of God, can't we get things straight?'

'Nothing could be straighter than the way things are now,' he pointed out callously.

'Why are you doing this?' she demanded

tearfully. 'Have I hurt you so badly that you need to punish me? I don't want a divorce, I don't want to be away from you—ever!'

He watched her speculatively, still drumming a devil's tattoo on the table. 'And what has produced this change of mind, my dear wife?'

She wanted so much to tell him she loved him more than anything on earth, wanted nothing more than to spend the rest of her life with him. But how could she say such words to a man whose Arctic eyes held not a trace of warmth? 'I—I've begun to see things more clearly now, Leo. I think I understand myself a little better now. And I understand you more, too. I now know you're not the monster I once imagined. And I feel such—such . . .' she fumbled for the words, 'such respect and admiration for you.'

'Respect?' He dismissed the word contemptuously. 'That's what a soldier shows his officer, Sabrina. As a basis for marriage, it's not enough.'

'Love, then——' she said desperately.

'Don't be a damned fool,' he snarled. 'You're rapidly becoming tedious. You've hated me from the start, woman. And you did your best to make me hate you, too.'

'No!'

'*Yes*,' he contradicted her, standing up. 'And you've succeeded. You've got what you wanted—now you must stick with it, I'm afraid. You and I will be much happier apart, anyway. This marriage was a gamble that didn't pay off. Let's leave it at that.'

Sabrina sat in dazed silence as he strolled out. He hadn't even listened to her, hadn't wanted to.

He hated her! Now she knew that there was no way out, no solution to her private tragedy.

Too shaken even to weep, she found her anorak, pulled it on, and ran out of the villa towards the stables. She needed speed, needed to fly from the unbearable pain that was going to destroy her.

Criterion was waiting for her in the stable, his fine, dark eyes rolling a little nervously as she heaved the saddle on to his back. It was cold, and her fingers fumbled with the buckles. Leading the big stallion out into the open, her mind flashed through other occasions when she had ridden Criterion. At Winfields one Sunday morning. And again, later, on that midnight when she had first learned that Leo wanted to marry her.

How much had changed since then, how much had gone wrong with her life!

Criterion's flanks shuddered in the cold. She fumbled her foot into the stirrup, and clambered on to his broad back. Oh Leo, Leo, she cried inside, if only you knew how much I loved you . . .

It was a blessed relief to be on the beach again, free to gallop where she chose. She even welcomed the wind that swept through her hair, chilling her face till it ached. The sea was grey, flecked with white, and the lowering winter sky promised more snow later on. Heedless, she gave Criterion his head, and the stallion swept along the beach, his flying hooves spurting up sand at every long stride.

It was over. The long, sweet dream was over. No more nights in the golden bed, no more days with the man she had first come to fear, then to love. The strange journey that had begun when he had first taken her hostage was now finally coming to an end.

The reins had rubbed Criterion's neck into a lather by the time she slowed down, panting in the icy air. What did the future hold now? A cold widowhood—she could think of it as nothing else—among ghostly memories? She knew that she would never be able to forget him. Leonardo l'Aquila had burned a track into her heart and mind that could never be eradicated.

She rode for a long time, her mind whirling with unconnected thoughts, and then headed back towards the villa. It was only when she noticed the dark wood to the right of the path that she realised she had come the wrong way. This path was the dangerous one. She reined the stallion in and paused for a moment, wondering whether to turn back. In her emotion, she had galloped the wrong way down the beach. To turn back now and go the other way round would take at least three quarters of an hour—and Criterion was already tired, his nostrils puffing clouds of steam into the cold air.

Making up her mind, she urged him on. She would just have to be careful, that was all.

The path narrowed towards the edge of the cliff, the dense, dark mass of the woods pressing her towards the brink. The crumbling side of the cliff was coming up now, and she leaned forward to shield the horse's eye from the drop, as she had done before. Sabrina found, rather to her dismay that her heart was pounding. Why? She had negotiated this place successfully twice before, after all.

The drop yawned giddily down to her left, and she clucked soothingly to the horse as he picked his way across the uneven ground, aware that danger was in the air. And then the earth gave way under Criterion's hooves, and he started, his big muscles shuddering with terror.

'Come on, boy,' she urged him, dry-mouthed, and he scrambled on. The slide of loose rocks and pebbles under his hooves became a sudden avalanche, and he staggered sickeningly on the edge. Clasping at his strong black neck, Sabrina took her hand away from his rolling eye—and as he suddenly saw the hideous drop beside him, the big horse reared up on to his hind legs in fear, whinnying. She screamed once as she felt herself sliding off his back, and she grasped ineffectually at the saddle.

In her thoughtlessness, she hadn't fastened the buckle properly, and the saddle pulled loose.

For a moment, her foot caught in the stirrup; and then Criterion surged forward with a deep grunt of terror, scrambling up over the collapsing ground—and Sabrina crashed heavily on to the gravel, slithered to the edge of the cliff—and fell.

Slowly, consciousness returned to her. It was bitter cold, colder than she had ever been, and a throbbing agony darted along her shoulders and spine as she tried to move. She opened her eyes, wincing at the pain, and stirred her legs slightly.

The clatter of falling gravel made her freeze in sudden terror.

She was lying on a ledge a dozen feet or so down from the top of the cliff. By some miracle, it had broken her fall. The pain in her shoulders exploded as she tried to crawl closer to the icy stone. Glancing downwards, her hair stirred in horror—beneath her was a sheer drop of several hundred feet to the beach below. As she turned her face, shuddering, to the cliff, her mind registered that there was no brown body at the bottom. Criterion must have got away, then. Grateful for that, at least, she tried to cradle her aching shoulder—it felt as though it was broken—and allowed herself to slip back into a half-faint. Sooner or later, she thought distantly, she would slip off this tiny refuge; and then her body would plummet down through the air to be shattered on the rocks far below. Her brain was so numb that the thought hardly affected her at all . . .

When she regained consciousness again, it was growing dark. The sun was setting in a dirty yellow smear across the sea, and the bitter cold had increased. In a half-dream, she was aware of Leo's voice calling her.

'Sabrina—don't move! I'm coming down to you!' That was impossible, she thought dimly. Leo was far away—she had never entertained the idea that he would come for her. It was a dream.

But a scatter of pebbles around her made her rouse herself with an effort.

'*Don't move!*'

The urgency in his voice penetrated her fuzzy

thoughts, and she lay back, grateful that the
agony in her shoulders and spine had dulled to a
heavy throb. Squinting upward, she could see a
man clambering down the cliff-face towards her.
At first she thought it must be some strange
hallucination; and then she noticed the nylon
rope with which he was belaying himself. It was
Leo.

A surge of joy rose in her heart, like a fresh
stream melting the ice. He had come for her!

'Leo,' she called to him, her throat dry and
parched, 'for God's sake be careful!'

'Just keep still,' he panted. With another
shower of flints, he lowered himself on to her
ledge, and then was stooping over her, his eyes
intent.

'Are you hurt?'

'My back,' she whispered, clasping at his arms
with weak fingers. 'Oh, thank God you came,
darling——'

'Your back?' he cut in, his face worried. 'How
bad is it?'

'Don't know—I must have—have landed on
my shoulders. Feels as though something's
broken—it hurts——'

'If it hurts, at least it's not broken,' he
commented tersely. 'But it could be tricky. Can
you move your hips and legs?'

'Numb,' she whispered, her eyes fluttering
closed.

'God,' she heard him mutter, and a faint smile
crossed her pale face.

'Sorry,' she muttered. 'I should have listened
to you about that path . . . stubborn, as usual.'

'Never mind that,' he said quietly. 'I'm going to lift you up, Sabrina. Just tell me exactly where and when it hurts. Okay?'

She nodded slightly, then gasped with pain as he lifted her off the rock, his powerful arms gentle and firm. She managed to suppress her whimpering until she was cradled against his broad chest. She lay there, her cold face pressed against the warmth of his skin, her lips close to his ear.

'I'm so glad you came, Leo,' she whispered. She felt the big muscles of his shoulders bunch as he began to haul them up the rope with his right hand, his left holding her tight against him. Absently, she registered his grunt of effort, the clatter of loose rocks skittering down the void beneath.

'I love you,' she told him between gasps. 'I always—have done. I wonder if you know that—if you'll ever know?'

He made no answer, and she lay limp in the crook of his arm as he heaved the double weight up the rope, his boots scraping at the crumbling rock.

After a few minutes, he paused to rest, and she was numbly aware that his chest was heaving, his breath coming in ragged gasps.

'Are you—all right?' she slurred out, trying to open her eyes. Her head was splitting, and a horrible sense of unreality had taken grip of her. She did not know it, but shock and concussion were taking their toll.

'Just relax,' he grunted. 'Only a few more feet to go.'

She tried to cling to him with broken-nailed fingers. 'Haven't you any one to help you?' she asked painfully.

'Couldn't wait for help. Sent—groom for—the doctor——'

His feet lost their grip, and they crashed against the rock. The sickening jar to her shoulders forced a low cry from Sabrina.

'Sorry,' Leo breathed, his muscles straining as he forced his way back up the rope. He did not speak again as he clawed himself up the final few feet—and then he was crawling over the crumbling edge of the cliff, dragging her as gently as he could after him. The jolting pains to her back shook her cruelly into wakefulness.

'Are we safe?' she panted, clinging to him as he lay still, his chest heaving.

'Yes,' he told her between great gasps for air, 'safe now.' He crawled to his feet after a few minutes and lifted her clumsily into his arms. 'Safe now, my love.'

Through a haze of pain, Sabrina was dimly conscious of the next few hours. Leo was with her in the ambulance that drove to the hospital, and she was dimly aware of his deep voice among the other voices that conferred about her in the brightly-lit theatre which hurt her eyes.

Numbly, she answered questions about her injuries, tried to respond as they asked her to move her legs, her toes. Expert fingers probed her back, sending stars of agony dancing in front of her eyes. At last she felt a needle slide into her skin, a tiny pain almost unnoticeable among all the other pains—and then a sweet relief spread through her upper body. She heard Leo's voice in her ear, felt his hand soothing her forehead.

'Your shoulder is dislocated,' he told her quietly. 'They're going to put it back now. Please hold on.'

The sudden pressure against her arm was apalling.

Despite the anaesthetic, she felt as though her body was being torn in two. The pain invaded her body, threatening to force her out of it by sheer pressure, and with disbelieving horror, she could feel bones grating deep in her flesh. She was unable to cry out. And then with a grinding click, she felt the socket slide home—and the pain receded into blackness.

But just before she passed out, she felt Leo's lips kiss hers with infinite tenderness.

He was still there when she awoke briefly around dawn, her hand firmly clasped in his. She tried to smile at him, and he stroked her cheek without speaking until she drifted back into a welcoming darkness again. She awoke for a second time during the morning, some hours later. It was bright and very quiet, and Leo was dozing by her bedside. His cheeks and chin were dark with beard, and she studied his tired face dreamily, loving him, until she herself fell back into a light doze.

By late afternoon, she had regained consciousness fully. Leo's dark grey eyes were on her, his smile softening the harsh lines of fatigue in his face.

'How are you feeling?'

'Much better,' she said. Her body felt very

weak. 'Does my arm have to be strapped up like this? It hurts.'

'Badly?'

'I suppose I'll live,' she said drily. 'At least I don't feel so horribly sick all the time.'

'The concussion did that.' His hand held hers firmly, his thumb caressing the satiny skin on the back of her hand. 'That was quite a trick you pulled,' he went on gently. 'That ledge was only a couple of feet wide, you know.'

'It was a very hard ledge,' she answered ruefully. 'It felt as though it had broken my back!'

'There's some very spectacular bruising,' he informed her, 'but nothing serious, thank God. If you hadn't landed on that ledge. Sabrina, you would have——' He broke off, his eyes dark.

'I wouldn't be here now,' she supplied, glancing timidly at the tautness of his face. 'Leo, I'm so terribly sorry! I should have listened to you about that path——'

'Hush,' he said gently, touching her lips with tender fingers. 'It's all over now—and thank heaven you've been spared.'

'Thank you for staying with me,' she sighed. 'I was terrified.'

'Just rest,' he soothed. 'I'll tell the doctors you're awake—they'll want to take a look at you.'

'How soon can I leave hospital, Leo?'

'Probably tonight. All you need now is rest— lots of rest. You've had a slight concussion, so you'll have to take it very easy.' He smiled warmly at her. 'But I'll see to that. Now lie still— I'm going to call the doctors.'

Later, Sara came to see her, bringing a huge box of expensive chocolates.

'You've given us quite a scare, *cara*,' she said reprovingly. 'When your horse came galloping back without his saddle, Leo knew exactly what had happened, thank God. He got the ropes, and went straight down to the cliff-edge. He risked his life to save you, you know.'

'I know,' Sabrina nodded. It was still a source of wonder to her. 'He won't have Criterion shot, will he?' she asked anxiously. Sara's eyes widened.

'But of course not. Besides, if the horse hadn't come back to tell us something was wrong, you might not be here now.' She unwrapped a chocolate and popped it deftly into Sabrina's mouth. 'How's the shoulder now?'

'Sore,' Sabrina admitted, 'but not bad.'

'Well it's all over now. The doctors say you can go home tonight if you want.'

'I'm so glad,' she smiled tiredly. 'Though I'm rather enjoying being made a fuss of!'

'Don't worry,' Leo's voice came from the doorway. 'There'll be plenty of that.' He came to sit on the other side of the bed and stroked her black hair away from her pale face. His eyes were smiling. 'The doctors have another battery of tests lined up—just to make completely sure— and then we can go home. Okay?'

'Okay,' she whispered happily. 'That sounds wonderful.'

It was good to be back home, back in her own bed and in her husband's arms. By the next morning, Sabrina felt recovered enough to get out of bed, and in the face of Dalila's concerned cluckings, she wrapped her still-weak body in a warm gown, and pottered around the house.

Her shoulder ached now and then, and would probably do so for a couple of days to come; but apart from the bruises on her back, she had come through her flirtation with death miraculously unscathed.

She had spent the night cradled in Leo's arms, utterly secure against the broad expanse of his chest, his steady heartbeat lulling her to peaceful sleep.

With daylight, other memories had returned.

This heaven was going to end very soon. Within a day or so, she was going to be well enough to travel—and then the divorce would be set in motion.

Hugging her hurt arm, she curled up in one of the window-seats, wrapped in a rug, and stared out across the wintry sea below. To leave all this was going to be the hardest thing she had ever done. It crossed her mind with sad irony that she had only seen Capri in winter! Within a very few weeks it was going to be spring, and the island would once more don the brilliant colours of Mediterranean sunlight. And by then she would be far away. The thought of going back to Winfields horrified her; she couldn't, she decided, ever go back there. She would sell the gloomy old mansion with its memories of her father, and find a cottage somewhere in the country.

What an empty life it would be! How devoid of colour, of warmth and joy! She had fancied herself unhappy on Capri—in fact, these had been the happiest months of her life. And now she was going to taste real unhappiness again, an unhappiness as deep and as lasting as that she had known as a child——

A gentle touch at her shoulder made her look up. Leo settled himself into the seat next to her, his tanned face tender.

'What sad thoughts are you thinking?' he asked in a velvety voice that made her stomach quiver.

'Oh—just about going back to England. What I'm going to do with the rest of my life—that sort of thing.'

His caress was feather-light against her cheek.

'You're not going back to England, Sabrina,' he said softly. Were the words a reprieve? She stared at him with wide blue eyes, her lips trembling. 'I mean that I owe you an apology, Sabrina—an apology that I don't think I'll ever be able to make properly. All that talk of divorce—it was just fiction. I never meant a syllable of it.'

She stared a few seconds longer as the words sank in, then gasped out a laugh that was half a sob.

'Oh, darling,' she choked, 'I love you so much . . .'

'I know,' he said softly, taking her in his arms with tenderness. 'I've known for weeks that you loved me but you didn't know it yourself. I could see you fighting against the knowledge, and so I decided to try and shock you into admitting it to yourself. God help me, I thought that if I threatened to divorce you, you'd realise what your real feelings were . . .'

'Then—you really never meant it?' she asked, closing her eyes against the hot tears that were ready to spill with joy.

'How could I mean it? I only wanted to make you accept your love for me—and mine for you. My darling, you're my whole life! I love you, Sabrina—I've loved you for months, planned and waited for you to love me in return . . .'

'I was so convinced that you hated me,' she said numbly. 'I couldn't believe you could have any other feeling for me!'

'Hate you?' He laughed, drawing closer. 'From the first moment I saw you, I knew I had to have you—you obsessed me, with your icy beauty, your poise, your coolness! I knew I had to melt you in my fire.'

'Then—you didn't marry me in order to humiliate me?' she faltered.

'Little goose! I married you because I loved you.' His lips sealed the statement against hers. 'I came to London months ago with the specific intention of smashing Westlake, yes. I was half-mad then, Sabrina, mad with wounds. I think you've guessed that. All I could think of was evening the score, getting my own back on Simon Westlake—as though that could have done any good!'

'I can't blame you,' she said quietly. 'I understand, Leo.'

'No—it was wrong, my darling wife. It was crazy. But it led me to you.' He smiled quietly, tracing the delicate line of her cheekbone with one finger. 'When I heard of your father's death, I was enraged—God forgive me. My great revenge had been snatched away from me! Then I remembered that Simon Westlake had left a daughter. I was consumed with curiosity. I had to see you, see what sort of woman you were. But to see you was to feel the strongest compulsion, the most powerful attraction, that I'd ever known.'

'Oh, Leo . . .'

'I found myself at a crossroad in my life, perhaps the most important crossroad of them all. All my feelings of hate for Simon Westlake had begun to evaporate. Instead I found a passion infinitely more worthwhile, infinitely stronger. My love for you. My love that was at first curiosity, then fascination, then obsession! God knows it wasn't easy. When wounds heal, they torment you, goad you into agony. I'd dreamed of this revenge for so long that giving it up was like admitting weakness. For a long while I trembled between the two, trying to stop love from conquering hate. But love conquers all things.' He shook his head slowly, a smile brooding on his mouth. 'And the love I felt for you was stronger than any hate could ever be.'

'Love conquered all things with me,' she said gently. 'Because for a time I almost hated you, too, Leo.'

'Yes. I know. Thank God for love.' He was still smiling. 'Not that I exactly welcomed it at the time. It was a great shock for me to have to admit that I was no longer self-sufficient. That I was no longer the lone wolf, but only half a personality. From now on I was going to need you at my side, to make me whole. Without you, I couldn't exist. That wasn't easy to admit, either! The trouble was I couldn't think of any way to get close to you, Sabrina. Wealth is a remarkable defender of privacy. You were always locked up in Winfields, or in limousines, escorted by the old men of Westlake. And more, you were so cold, so distant—I knew that even if I did get through to you, you would probably simply turn away, protected by your icy mantle. That made me desperate—and desperate men do desperate things! I couldn't take the chance of wooing you—and perhaps losing you. There was no choice but to capture you by force or guile. The means were to hand. The campaign I'd set up against your father would be equally efficient against his daughter. By doing what I had planned to do in the first place, conquering Westlake, I would be able to conquer you.'

'I can scarcely believe it,' she sighed, still tearful as she gazed up into his eyes. 'I learned to love you very early on, Leo. But you were always distant with me, letting me imagine that you wanted to hurt me and make me suffer . . .'

'I think you've suffered enough, Sabrina,' he said quietly. 'I was trying to find a way of breaking that prison of ice around you—and every time I hurt you, my own heart bled. Especially that night in Naples. God, how I survived that I'll never know.'

'Nor will I,' she said, shaking her head at the terrible memory. 'I don't think I've ever cried so much.'

'I swear that I'm going to make sure you never shed another tear as long as you live,' he smiled.

'I couldn't be happier than I am now, Leo,' she whispered. 'Nothing could make me more complete.'

'There is something else,' he said, his smile fading. 'Something important I have to tell you.'

'What is it?' she asked, made anxious by his seriousness.

'The hospital 'phoned through this morning with the results of one of the tests they did on you.'

'Tests?' she queried, looking into his eyes. 'Which one?'

'A very important one,' he said gravely. 'You're pregnant, my love. They asked me some questions about you—and they say you're probably going to have a baby in about eight months' time, around midsummer.'

'Are you serious?' she asked, stunned by the news.

'Very serious.' He smiled slightly. 'Though it's usually the wife who breaks the news to the husband.' He touched her face, and she realised that for the first time in her life she was seeing him worried. 'How do you feel about it, Sabrina?'

'About the baby?' She laughed from sheer joy, kissing him. 'I think it's the most wonderful news I've ever heard!'

'Oh, my love!' He leaned back, his eyes squeezed shut. 'Thank God for that. If you only knew how I've worried since this morning!'

'Because I once said I'd never have your child?' Her own eyes were wet. 'Leo, I've said some

crazy things to you, and that was one of the
craziest of all. I'm going to have all the sons and
daughters you can give me, my love. Starting
midsummer.'

The expression on his face gave her all the
answer she needed. Adoringly, he swept her up in
his arms.

'We're going to bed,' he said firmly. 'You need
plenty of rest.'

'You don't look as though you've got rest in
mind,' she laughed, flushing hotly as he laid her
gently on the bed.

He kissed away the remaining tears from her
lashes before kissing her mouth in a declaration
of love that wiped all other thoughts from her
mind. Unhurriedly, he began unfolding her robe
to reveal the satiny perfection of her skin.

'God, you're beautiful,' he said in a husky sigh,
and she found that her hands were shaking as
they explored the warm velvet of his chest under
his shirt.

'Leo,' she gasped, as his lips touched her skin.
'My Leo. Don't ever leave me . . .'

'I never will,' he whispered. She half-opened
languorous eyes as his lips began to find the
sweetest, most sensitive places on her body.

'The doctor said I had to be careful of my
shoulder,' she teased him softly.

'Oh,' he promised her silkily 'you'll be amazed
at just how gentle I can be . . .'

You're invited to accept 4 books and a surprise gift **Free!**

Acceptance Card

Mail to: **Harlequin Reader Service®**

In the U.S.
2504 West Southern Ave.
Tempe, AZ 85282

In Canada
P.O. Box 2800, Postal Station A
5170 Yonge Street
Willowdale, Ontario M2N 6J3

YES! Please send me 4 free Harlequin Romance® novels and my free surprise gift. Then send me 6 brand new novels every month as they come off the presses. Bill me at the low price of $1.65 each ($1.75 in Canada)—an 11% saving off the retail price. There are no shipping, handling or other hidden costs. There is no minimum number of books I must purchase. I can always return a shipment and cancel at any time. Even if I never buy another book from Harlequin, the 4 free novels and the surprise gift are mine to keep forever.

116 BPR-BPGE

Name _____ (PLEASE PRINT)

Address _____ Apt. No. _____

City _____ State/Prov. _____ Zip/Postal Code _____

This offer is limited to one order per household and not valid to present subscribers. Price is subject to change.   ACR-SUB-1

Experience the warmth of…

Harlequin Romance

The original romance novels.
Best-sellers for more than 30 years.

Delightful and intriguing love stories
by the world's foremost writers
of romance fiction.

Be whisked away to dazzling
international capitals…
or quaint European villages.
Experience the joys of falling in love…
for the first time, the best time!

Harlequin Romance

A uniquely absorbing journey
into a world of superb romance reading.

Wherever paperback books are sold, or through
Harlequin Reader Service

In the U.S.	In Canada
2504 West Southern Avenue	P.O. Box 2800, Postal Station A
Tempe, AZ 85282	5170 Yonge Street
	Willowdale, Ontario M2N 6J3

No one touches the heart of a woman
quite like Harlequin!

R-111

EYE OF THE STORM

MAURA SEGER

A powerful
portrayal of
the events of
World War II in the
Pacific, *Eye of the Storm* is a riveting story of how love
triumphs over hatred. In this, the first of a three-book
chronicle, Army nurse Maggie Lawrence meets Marine
Sgt. Anthony Gargano. Despite military regulations
against fraternization, they resolve to face together
whatever lies ahead.... Author Maura Seger, also known
to her fans as Laurel Winslow, Sara Jennings, Anne
MacNeil and Jenny Bates, was named 1984's
Most Versatile Romance Author by *The Romantic Times*.

At your favorite bookstore in April or send your name, address and zip or
postal code, along with a check or money order for $4.25 (includes 75¢ for
postage and handling) payable to Harlequin Reader Service to:

HARLEQUIN READER SERVICE
In the U.S.
Box 52040
Phoenix, AZ 85072-2040

In Canada
5170 Yonge Street
P.O. Box 2800
Postal Station A
Willowdale, Ont. M2N 6J3

EYE-E-1

You're invited to accept 4 books and a surprise gift Free!

Acceptance Card

Mail to: **Harlequin Reader Service®**

In the U.S.
2504 West Southern Ave.
Tempe, AZ 85282

In Canada
P.O. Box 2800, Postal Station A
5170 Yonge Street
Willowdale, Ontario M2N 6J3

YES! Please send me 4 free Harlequin Presents® novels and my free surprise gift. Then send me 8 brand new novels every month as they come off the presses. Bill me at the low price of $1.75 each ($1.95 in Canada)—an 11% saving off the retail price. There are no shipping, handling or other hidden costs. There is no minimum number of books I must purchase. I can always return a shipment and cancel at any time. Even if I never buy another book from Harlequin, the 4 free novels and the surprise gift are mine to keep forever.   108 BPP-BPGE

Name _____ (PLEASE PRINT) _____

Address _____ Apt. No. _____

City _____ State/Prov. _____ Zip/Postal Code _____

This offer is limited to one order per household and not valid to present subscribers. Price is subject to change.   ACP-SUB-1

PASSIONATE!
CAPTIVATING!
SOPHISTICATED!

Harlequin Presents...

**The favorite fiction
of women the world over!**

Beautiful contemporary romances that
touch every emotion of a woman's heart—
passion and joy, jealousy and heartache...
but most of all...love.

Fascinating settings in the exotic
reaches of the world—
from the bustle of an international capital
to the paradise of a tropical island.

**All this and much, much more
in the pages of**

Harlequin Presents...

Wherever paperback books are sold, or through
Harlequin Reader Service

In the U.S.
2504 West Southern Avenue
Tempe, AZ 85282

In Canada
P.O. Box 2800, Postal Station A
5170 Yonge Street
Willowdale, Ontario M2N 6J3

**No one touches the heart of a woman
quite like Harlequin!**

P-111

Just what the woman on the go needs!

BOOKMATE

The perfect "mate" for all Harlequin paperbacks!

Holds paperbacks open for hands-free reading!

- **TRAVELING**
- **VACATIONING**
- **AT WORK • IN BED**
- **COOKING • EATING**
- **STUDYING**

Perfect size for all standard paperbacks, this wonderful invention makes reading a pure pleasure! Ingenious design holds paperback books OPEN and FLAT so even wind can't ruffle pages—leaves your hands free to do other things. Reinforced, wipe-clean vinyl-covered holder flexes to let you turn pages without undoing the strap...supports paperbacks so well, they have the strength of hardcovers!

Snaps closed for easy carrying.

Available now. Send your name, address, and zip or postal code, along with a check or money order for just $4.99 + .75¢ for postage & handling (for a total of $5.74) payable to Harlequin Reader Service to:

Harlequin Reader Service

In the U.S.A.
2504 West Southern Ave.
Tempe, AZ 85282

In Canada
P.O. Box 2800, Postal Station A
5170 Yonge Street,
Willowdale, Ont. M2N 5T5

MATE-1R